Lazarus Rising

Also by Joseph Caldwell

Novels

In Such Dark Places
The Deer at the River
Under the Dog Star
The Uncle from Rome
Bread for the Baker's Child
The Pig Did It
The Pig Comes to Dinner
The Pig Goes to Hog Heaven

Nonfiction

In the Shadow of the Bridge

Theater

The Bridge
Clay for the Statues of Saints
Cockeyed Kite
The Downtown Holy Lady
The King and the Queen of Glory

Lazarus

Rising

a novel by

Joseph Caldwell

Delphinium Books

Printed in the United States of America

For information, address
DELPHINIUM BOOKS, INC.,
16350 Ventura Boulevard, Suite D
PO Box 803
Encino, CA 91436

Library of Congress Cataloging-in-Publication Data is
available on request.
ISBN 978-1-883285-99-9
20 21 22 LSC 10 9 8 7 6 5 4 3 2 1

First Edition

Book Design by Colin Dockrill, AIGA

To

William Gale Gedney

In loving memory

"Though nothing can bring back of hour
Of the splendor in the grass . . ." —William Wordsworth,
"Ode: Intimations of Immortality"

Do not go gentle into that good night,
Rage, rage against the dying of the light

—Dylan Thomas

Prologue

Dempsey Coates first met Johnny Donegan the night the Haviland Piano Factory burned, all six floors of it. There had been no Haviland pianos made in the building for over fifty years, but the light industry that took over the loft spaces lacked sufficient individuality to offer an identity that might replace the superseded pianos. Even after the gutted shell was rebuilt and occupied by artists, sculptors, lawyers, and psychiatrists, it would be known as the Piano Factory.

Dempsey did not live in the Piano Factory. She lived down the block on the other side of the street, the uptown side, in a building with no name, with no particular history.

Coming home from a gallery opening, she'd had to retrace her steps back to Varick Street, go around the block, and come to her building from the other direction, from the west. Her own street was blocked by what was called the "apparatus": fire engines, ladders, chiefs' cars, an ambulance, and enough crisscrossing hose to map the entire Northeast.

In spite of the nipping cold, Dempsey had walked down from Prince Street, across Canal to Tribeca, reveling in her defiance of the winter weather, refusing to hunch her shoulders, to draw her arms protectively against her sides, to shiver or to shake. Her head she held high so the wind could have its way against her chin, her neck. The thick woolen scarf, a greenish brown, she'd knitted it for her best friend, Winnie, then decided to keep it for herself—was allowed to warm her chest, but her face must be kept open to the elements, an eager participant in the crisp iced air that made taut her skin, numbed her lips and all but cauterized her eyes.

Rather than be annoyed by the enforced detour, she lifted her head even higher, amused that her encounter with the winter night would now be prolonged. Out the cloudy breaths came; more joyfully defiant was her sure step onto the granulated frost covering the pavement. She went to Varick, turned north for one block, made the turn to the west for two blocks, then south one block and back onto her own street. She stopped at the corner and took in the spectacle.

Klieg lights lit the entire scene as if someone were making a movie. Huge blasts of water shot skyward, sculpting gothic stalactites on the building's overhang, on the lintels and sills of the blown-out windows. A voice was heard on a loudspeaker, urgent, annoyed, the director trying to keep control of the action.

Helmeted firemen in cumbersome coats and gauntlet gloves and what looked like wading boots, only heavier, the kind favored by the Three Musketeers, were wandering in and out among the apparatus, stumbling on the hoses, some of the men carrying poles, some humping the hoses to feed out more line toward the ladders, others, faces blackened, the whites of their eyes seeming, in contrast, to be made of milk glass. The men traced their way along the hoses to other hoses that might or might not lead them to where they wanted to go.

Only the fire itself seemed organized. The Piano Factory had become a chimney, the roof completely opened, the flames rising, red orange mostly, a blacker red beneath, billowing skyward rather lazily, enjoying themselves, knowing that the worst was over—the blind snaking between walls, underneath floors, the fire's panicked attempt to find more air. Now the flames had found their way into the open sky. All would be well. They could breathe. They could take it easy; they could just rumble and roll themselves, great mounded billows, folding back into themselves, demonstrating what it really meant to be fire.

Four firemen were walking toward Dempsey. They were weaving, stumbling against each other, bumping shoulders, unsteadying themselves all the more. The man in the lead was using a pole of some kind—with a two-pronged hook at the tip—as a walking staff. One of his boots had flopped down to his calf and his helmet was tipped slightly to the side, an attempt, perhaps, at style. At each building they'd stop and the lead man would try the door. When it failed to yield, he'd pound on it, wait, and then they would all move on.

Dempsey heard one of them say, "They know we're here. They know we're freezing." The men stomped up the three steps onto what had been the docking platform of the building next to Dempsey's. After he'd yanked twice at the door, he pounded with his fist, then looked up at some lighted windows on the third floor. "We're freezing," he yelled. But his voice was caught up in the shouts, roars, and crashing from the burning building behind him.

Dempsey thought she should at least point out that there were six doorbells arrayed along the sides of the doors, each an independent installation that accommodated the occupied lofts inside. It then occurred to her that she herself had only to open her own door with her own key and the men would find warmth—or at least shelter, since the hallways of the building were unheated. Or she could invite them to her loft. If there was time, they could warm themselves, recover their strength and return to battle the blaze refreshed. Who could do less? She could make coffee. She was not, by nature, an easy host, but for four freezing and exhausted firemen she might be able to mutate into something more gracious.

"You looking for a place to warm up?"

"No," said one man standing slightly behind the others, "we're selling the Encyclopedia Britannica."

"All right then."

"Wait. Yes." The lead man's voice was more weary than repentant. "We've been relieved for a quick break. We're looking for a place to warm up."

"Well, you've come to the right place." Dempsey fiddled in her coat pocket for the keys. The clip of a Bic pen was caught in the key ring. She jiggled it free, then drew the keys out of the pocket. A roll of Certs dropped to the cement. No one stooped to pick it up. She put the key into the lock and opened the door. The metal scraped along the cement, the hinges whined, the door itself complaining of the cold.

By the time Dempsey had taken the key out of the lock, the firemen were inside. She retrieved the Certs, then closed the door behind her. The men had plopped themselves down onto the bottom steps of the wide stairway that led to the floors above. The lead man had set his staff against the wall and had lowered his head onto his crossed arms. The others leaned either against the wall or the stairway railing. They were breathing heavily as if they'd run rather than stumbled down the block. Gray mucous flowed from their nostrils, wetting the black soot on their chins, dripping down onto the clasps that held closed their rubber coats.

"You want to come upstairs? It's warmer there." Dempsey pulled the thick chain that would bring down the old freight elevator. The clanking and clattering began as if a full complement of galley slaves had been lashed into labor. The leader raised his head and drew his gloved hand over his ears, then let the hands fall back to his knees. "We're okay here," he said. "We don't have that long. But thanks." Some of the words were obliterated by the clanking elevator chains, but Dempsey thought she understood the meaning.

"I'll bring down some coffee. Black okay?"

"Sounds great," the man said.

The elevator, with a thump, arrived. Dempsey gave the upper half of the door a quick hoist, sending the lower half down into the floor. After she'd stepped inside and the door began to close, she saw that the man had lowered his head again onto his arms.

From the large pot that brewed endless amounts of coffee that she'd drink while spending long hours at her easel, Dempsey brought them down cups of it, not on a tray but on a piece of Plexiglas stained with paint, some of it in gobs, some in streaks that had washed into the other colors. It was, Dempsey explained, a palette. She was a painter. An artist. Their lack of interest in so fascinating a revelation might have annoyed her, but there was nothing much she was willing to do about it. A lecture on the importance of the artist in our society did not seem relevant under the circumstances.

Two of the cups were bone china, the other two, thick white mugs she'd swiped from a diner. The two men slumped against the wall chose the bone china; the men near the railing got the mugs. The man who'd done all the talking let himself be last. As he dug the spoon into the sugar bowl, Dempsey had to create an opposing upward pressure so the palette wouldn't be shoved all the way down to the floor. The man mumbled some thanks—at least she heard it as thanks—then took a strong gulp.

Dempsey waited for approval or complaint. The man was looking at her over the rim of his cup. He tilted the cup upward but could still see her around the sides of the mug. When she started to move away, he put a hand on her arm to keep her there. He lowered his mug and, still saying nothing, added another spoonful of sugar.

Dempsey set the palette onto the floor and poured more coffee into the smaller cups. She tried to bend mostly from the shoulders rather than the waist so she wouldn't be sticking out her behind. The presumed leader was now holding his mug up against his face, warming his cheek. He was still looking at her, and she became aware that his eyes were a deep and penetrating blue. She was more amused than flattered that she had become their favored object.

He lowered the mug and moved his gloved hand in a circular motion, swirling the coffee inside. Even though he seemed huge, garbed as he was in the enormous rubber coat, shod with the high and bulky boots and gloved with the gauntlets of a falconer, it seemed to Dempsey that she was looking at a sixteen-year-old who'd slipped down inside a fireman costume. Even the soot on the man's face failed to give him the toughness and texture the uniform seemed to demand. But the nose, smudged, smeared by an attempt that had been made to wipe away the mucous, could only be characterized as perfect. It was far from delicate, even somewhat obtrusive and yet perfect.

Dempsey purposely looked at the other men, eager

to pour more coffee if necessary—or offer more sugar if it was wanted. As she watched them gulping and heard their frequent sighs, she felt an odd sense of satisfaction. For her, for these brief moments, they had become her charges, a brood given to her care. She almost felt uneasy when she realized they had warmed her heart. They were the ones who gave. And she, somewhat to her amazement, was the grateful recipient. To distract her from the uneasiness she felt, she asked the man, "More sugar?"

Now looking directly at her, he said, "Thanks, but I'm fine."

The next meeting between Dempsey and Johnny was far less eventful. Johnny had stolen the sugar spoon. He'd slipped it inside his glove when Dempsey turned to give more coffee to the bone-china men. Two days after the fire he rang one of the bells outside the door to her building and was told by a man calling down from the third-floor window that the woman he was looking for—the artist lady with the honey-colored hair—was Dempsey Coates and her loft was on the sixth, the top, floor.

Johnny returned the spoon. First he said he had pocketed it by mistake; then he admitted it had been deliberate. He had wanted to see her again.

"A thief and a liar," Dempsey said. "And devious besides. What more could a woman want?"

This time the blue eyes neither flattered nor amused.

And so they were brought together, the fireman and the painter, Dempsey Coates, the artist from Manhattan, and Johnny Donegan, the youth from Staten Island. Added to the obvious excitement available to two young people was the exoticism they provided to each other. Dempsey felt, through Johnny, she was being brought into a world of valor and sacrifice. He was ordinary, but extraordinary; he was brave and he was good. He was like no one Dempsey had ever known or expected to know. And he was from Staten Island, a country she had visited but would never have claimed as her own. But now all this could be hers.

That Johnny would have for his lover the most desirable woman in the world and an artist besides, one who lived in a loft in Tribeca, was a possibility not even introduced to his most fantastic imaginings. And now, through her, he came into possession of a world more distant than Cathay, than Mozambique, than Manhattan itself. This world was never meant to be his. But now it was—for the taking.

Given the circumstances and the two people involved, none of this could possibly last. And it didn't. Within a few months, before summer had come and gone, the affair was at an end. At the beginning, Dempsey felt, Johnny had revealed himself to be a god. And she, in turn, became his idolater. She worshiped Johnny, and he, in amazement, accepted this elevation to divine status. Eagerly he received her offerings; lavishly he bestowed his gifts, never doubting that Dempsey had seen him for who and what he truly was. But Dempsey, like any mystic given to worship, to say nothing of abject adoration, could not sustain the intensity of her ecstatic state. She eventually decided that Johnny Donegan, despite his many splendors, was one man among many, not the singular idol she had worshipped, fireman or no fireman, Staten Island or no Staten Island. And besides, she was not yet ready to remove herself from a life of other possibilities. Her adoration ended, and she was quite simply no longer in love—hardly an unusual phenomenon—and there was nothing she could do about it. Nor did she feel required to even try. It was hardly Johnny's fault that he was no longer possessed of the mystery that once had so entranced her.

And so he withdrew with what grace this devastation would allow and did what he could not to cry out and gnash his teeth, to go mad and fall in a tangled heap.

In the years between Dempsey's first experience of Johnny and her second, he was mostly forgotten. She had her painting, her other men, then later, her drugs, and even later, her illness.

The money for the drugs came from her mother by way of a limousine service. The limousine had made a right turn off Third Avenue onto Twenty-Seventh Street. Her mother had been crossing Twenty-Seventh. The light was in her favor. The limousine hit her and killed her. To protect the names of the occupants, the limousine company's lawyer offered Dempsey six hundred thousand dollars, an out-of-court settlement. From the lawyer, she learned that at the time of the accident, an autopsy had shown that her mother was drunk. Dempsey's mother never drank. Her only delight was the horses. Alcohol, sex, drugs never had a chance.

Dempsey had considered finding her own lawyer, but when she discovered that he (or she) would claim from forty to fifty percent of her mother's hard-earned cash, Dempsey decided she'd try her own negotiating skills—emanating from an implacable streak of inborn stubbornness. She would take her chances. Her mother, she didn't doubt, would have approved.

The limousine lawyer showed her the obviously falsified autopsy report to make her aware of the power he had at his command, a power that reached even into the city morgue. The lawyer's offices were paneled with walnut that didn't look like veneer. The desk was teak and as smooth as a piece of driftwood that had crossed all seven seas and finally washed up on Madison Avenue; the spacious view from his office reached all the way to LaGuardia Airport. The man himself was slovenly, as if he'd cast himself in the part of a small-town lawyer, complete with rumpled suit, wrinkled collar, and too wide and garish a tie. He slouched in his chair, he peered at her over bifocals. Apparently it was all meant to reassure the clients or litigants that he was a wise, well-intentioned practitioner, eager to achieve simple justice with the least possible fuss. And she had to admit he was masterfully persuasive. With the simple gesture, the pudgy-fingered hand offering her the autopsy report, he had let her know that her mother's death had an importance to people who would prefer not to be made important themselves. Perjury and falsification that could reach into any level of litigation were common tools of his trade, tools that he could wield with big-hearted alacrity and deadly determination.

Partly to give the man a chance to revel in the exercise of his craft and partly to pay tribute to her mother's gambling instincts, Dempsey sat and pretended to ponder. With a show of innocence, she said perhaps a trial would be the better resolution of the situation. The lawyer did not object; he even seemed to indicate that he would be guided by nothing but her wishes. Then he mentioned, in passing, a man who had seen her mother stagger out into the street, not in the crosswalk but from behind a parked car. The limousine had tried to stop, but the lurch was too sudden, out of nowhere. No other witnesses seemed available even though the death took place at nine-twenty in the evening, a time when Third Avenue is hardly a deserted byway. Clearly the lawyer had resources and was not hesitant to use them to the full advantage of his client.

Dempsey simply sat and continued her presumed pondering. She put her hand to her mouth, then to her cheek, then used it to prop up her chin. She examined her elbow, rubbed it, then crossed her arms and lowered her head. The lawyer watched closely, as if he would be required at any moment to repeat, in sequence, every move and gesture Dempsey was performing. Dempsey thought of staring at the ceiling, but that would be too obvious even for her, to say nothing of the lawyer. Even though she faltered, she knew that thinking of all her mother had wanted for her—a career as a working artist, to be loved unconditionally, to be solvent—would allow her to hang on in what was clearly a game. The lawyer finally mentioned seven hundred thousand. Dempsey felt that an even million would be the more accurate validation of her negotiating skills. Through an extended series of silences, gestures, and shifts of the buttocks, a figure of eight hundred thousand was agreed upon, each of them protesting that wrongful sacrifices were being made.

Dempsey was, in fact, annoyed with herself for lacking the patience and fortitude to go for the million—a figure her mother had struggled toward all her life, following the horses from one track to the next to the next, coming if not close at least within distance of palpable encouragement. A measure of her dedication found expression in Dempsey's name. A tip from a friend one evening in the champion boxer Jack Dempsey's restaurant had paid munificently enough for her mother to commemorate the event by giving her one and only daughter a somewhat singular name for a girl. The girl loved her name and was forever grateful.

Then, too, with an extended run of her luck, her mother had sent Dempsey to an upstate convent school for two years, and an initiation into the art of painting. If the nuns made little impact with religious instruction, the attraction of art was more than compensatory. If heaven had passed her by during the distribution of faith and hope and charity, compensation had been made when looks and talent were being handed out. She was, from the beginning, a beauty—and she accepted it calmly, even gratefully. During her stay at Mount St. Ann, her gift for art became increasingly apparent, especially to Dempsey herself.

(She had found herself very much attracted to Sister Sarah's approach to painting. "To be an artist," Sister had said, "you must love mystery. The true purpose of the real is to lead the way to mystery—which is the ultimate reality. The purpose of an objective painting is to show that way, the way to mystery. If it doesn't, it's merely illustration. An abstract painting must be the mystery itself. If it isn't, it's merely decoration.")

When the eight hundred thousand was finally settled on, Dempsey was somewhat pleased that her mother's final earthly act had ended in an actual gamble—one that paid off. The only indication of the lawyer's feelings about the transaction was the repeated smoothing of his necktie. So involved was the good man in this gesture that Dempsey decided a handshake could be dispensed with. He was still soothing his tie when Dempsey left.

Dempsey's descent into drugs was driven by her painting. Not that she was blocked. Far from it. In fact, never had she painted better; never had inspiration and revelation cooperated so completely. Her excitement was unending. She wanted nothing but to work, to paint. But the mind, the body, couldn't keep up with her. Physical exhaustion would make its claims; mental fatigue, the refusal of the most common intellectual endeavor to go any further without intermission, would close down her mind, making it impossible for her to continue. But there was nothing she wanted to do until the intermission was over, whether it was an hour, an evening, a night, or whatever. She had concentration for nothing but her work. She wanted oblivion until the interval had ended. She wanted no life but painting. She wanted to be nothing and be nowhere unless she could pick up her brush and squeeze paint onto her palette.

She found the oblivion she so desperately needed in the Lunch Room, a communal neighborhood shooting-up gallery near the Financial District frequented mostly by Wall Street types—financiers, accountants, bankers, with a few lawyers and an occasional designer or decorator thrown in. There she could while away the unwanted hours. Except that, before she would admit to what was happening, the unwanted hours became the wanted ones, the painting abandoned, the unbearable excitements exchanged for even more unbearable cravings.

With the drugs, mostly main-line heroin, Dempsey became promiscuous—not because of an increased passion but because of a kind of indifference. If someone wanted to have sex with her, she knew of no reason to refuse. Without any sort of preference, she had no criteria for accepting or refusing. She was young, unable to judge for herself, she accepted the compliments that she was beautiful. It had occurred to her more than once that the men who approached her were motivated not by any great desire but by a wish to proclaim a conquest. They wanted credit for having seduced a beautiful young woman more than they wanted the woman herself.

When she began to have nausea as well as unusual

fatigue, Dempsey went to see her mother's physician, who ran some tests and told her she was pregnant. The news was a shock, but then she held firmly that for the sake of her unborn child, she would immediately make her recovery from drugs unaided. She would not even resort to the substitute legal drugs that might have eased her return to sobriety. Those, too, she felt, would affect the baby. What pangs and terrors of withdrawal she might experience would have to be considered symptoms of her pregnancy. The nausea, the cramps, the high-pitched voices she could hear scratching faintly in the walls—these were what a woman in her third month had to expect. When the shadows advanced toward her, when her body became giddy with fear, she would explain to herself that she was pregnant and all this would pass once the baby was born.

But the baby lived fewer than six hours.

To explain the child's death, the doctor reminded her of the HIV test she'd agreed to during her pregnancy. She had no memory of it. He reminded her that she had tested positive. She had no memory of that either. But that, the doctor explained, had caused the premature birth and speedy death.

Dempsey turned to stone. She was infected. She'd infected her son. He had died. But she was living. And she would be living with that knowledge, a knowledge that she vowed would never be ignored.

More than three years after they had parted, Dempsey and Johnny ran into each other on a brisk Saturday morning in the fall, on Church Street. Johnny was walking down to the Staten Island ferry; Dempsey was going to her friend Winnie's to see some of her new paintings.

Johnny saw Dempsey before she'd seen him and stopped. Dempsey noticed that a man headed toward her was now standing still, about fifteen feet away. When she saw that it was Johnny Donegan, she, too, stopped, but only for a moment, then continued toward him. He brushed his thumb across his chin, and then took the few steps that brought the two of them within about three feet of each other. Again they stopped. Both tried a twitching smile, then just stared.

Dempsey had forgotten Johnny's habit of opening his mouth slightly whenever he wasn't sure what he wanted to say. Johnny saw that her hair was shorter and that her uncovered left ear was still the most delicate and tender formation of flesh ever created. They exchanged greetings. Dempsey told Johnny she was on her way to Winnie's. Johnny told her he was headed for the Staten Island ferry. When he asked about her painting, she said the expected thing, that it was going well, then mentioned the series of Lazarus paintings she had wanted to do as a memorial to her friend Jamey, who had died. Jamey was to have been the model. Johnny, after closing then parting his lips, offered to be the model. Dempsey told him she had AIDS. Unblinking, Johnny again closed his lips, parted them, once, twice, and lifted his chin ever so slightly. He repeated the offer. She accepted it warily.

At first their relationship pretended to be determinedly professional. Then, while painting *Lazarus Afflicted*, with his sisters Martha and Mary, Dempsey had a case of the sweats. Usually the sweats came at night, but this was mid-morning. She tried to ignore them, even though huge drops were falling on the shirt she was wearing. Johnny suggested a break. She refused. Then she fainted. When she came to, Johnny was brushing the hair from her forehead. Her teeth began to chatter and she could feel that the sweat had soaked through the shirt, with large wet splotches sticking to her back. She sat up and pulled her knees against her stomach. Her whole body was shaking. Johnny put a blanket across her shoulders and drew it around her, doubling it in front and making sure it covered her feet. He tucked it more tightly at the neck, then drew his hand away.

"I'm going to call the doctor," he said.

"No. Not necessary. It'll pass. I just have to—I have to try not to—not to rattle myself to pieces."

"Then you'd better go lie down."

"Let me stop shaking first. I will in a little—a little while."

After checking the front fold of the blanket, Johnny stayed where he was, on one knee, watching her. He placed one arm behind her, beneath her shoulders, and put his other arm across so he could pull her gently toward himself. She let herself be held against him. And so, again, they became lovers.

1.

In St. Patrick's Cathedral for the annual firefighters' mass, Johnny occupied himself before the celebration by following the narrative in the stained-glass windows of the north transept, high above the massive doors that led out to Fifty-First Street. He'd already looked at the Adoration of the Magi, the central panel, and had decided to go back to the beginning, starting with the Angel's Annunciation in the lower left-hand corner. Now Johnny was looking at St. Joseph, asleep and dreaming, while yet another angel explained to him that his pregnant bride had conceived of the Holy Spirit, which meant that there was really nothing for him to worry about. St. Joseph's robe seemed made of poured maple syrup; the angel clothed in the spun colors of a key-lime pie. (Johnny had not yet had breakfast.) It pleased him that what was a somewhat complicated situation in the relationship between Joseph and his wife Mary was being clarified at last. God was making the man privy to his inscrutable ways and now his married life could proceed as planned. Johnny liked the idea that God had the history, if not the habit, of making disclosures that could calm and console. There was an explanation for everything and God proved to be quite capable of dispensing insights when it suited his purposes. There was comfort in this truth, but before it could invade his spirit, the fireman in front of him slid back up onto his pew, hitting the joined knuckles Johnny had folded in an attitude of prayer.

Because this was a lieutenant and Johnny was only a regular firefighter, he, too, slid up onto his seat, taking into his spine the knuckled fist of the man behind him. The knuckles immediately withdrew and the shuffle of shoes, the swish of cloth indicated that the chain reaction set in motion by the lieutenant was now progressing behind him, probably getting the firefighters off their knees in a straight line that reached to the back of the cathedral.

It was time for Johnny to sit down anyway. He hadn't been praying. He had made no real effort to concentrate, to collect himself and his thoughts and direct them toward the divine presence into whose company he'd come. He wasn't sure he wanted to be there, even though he'd planned to attend and had prepared for it, rehearsed the role he'd decided to play: he would, in his wrath, confront the cardinal in his very own cathedral. The day before, his parish priest on Staten Island had told him he could not allow Dempsey and him to marry. When making love, Johnny had to use a condom. If he didn't, he'd get AIDS. But the condom meant that his sperm could not go calling on Dempsey's ova. The consummating marriage act would be thwarted, the marriage itself invalid. It could not, therefore, be allowed in the first place.

At communion time, Johnny would make known his anger, in person, to the cardinal—not because he expected a revision of canon law, but because he wanted His Eminence to be duly shamed by the injustice of hierarchical rigidities and made aware that the whole issue of condoms in the AIDS epidemic was not limited to gays but affected straights as well, and decorated ones at that, firefighters of known valor like John Francis Donegan who surely deserved better from the Church to which he had given allegiance all the days of his life. He was that mad. But he had an even greater concern than confronting the Cardinal: Dempsey's need for him at home, at this very hour, this very minute. Here he was, indulging himself in some petulant exercise, while Dempsey might still be wincing in pain with no one there to help her.

Just as he had been about to leave the loft for the cathedral, Dempsey had been gripped by a severe case of cramps. It had seized not only her stomach, but her legs, mostly her calves. Ordinarily she would have given no indication of the pain she was suffering, but it was difficult for her to deny that she was bent forward in her walk and that she had to grimace between words. The repeated wincing finally forced her to admit she was having some difficulty. After a sudden spasm had pulled her upward on her way to the kitchen sink, she sat down, leaned over and began to rub the calf of her right leg.

"Here, let me," Johnny had said. He squatted down in front of her and placed his hand on the back of her leg. "Slow or fast?"

"Try medium. Medium fast."

Johnny cupped her heel in the palm of his left hand and began rubbing with his right. "The other one too?" He asked.

"This one first," Dempsey whispered. She leaned her head back and stared at the ceiling. Johnny raised her leg so that her ankle fit into his shoulder bone. With both hands he rubbed the leg, applying as much pressure as he could without slowing the movement of his hands. "Better?"

"Not yet."

"Tell me when to do the other one."

"Yeah. I will."

His wrists began to tire, to cramp up, but still he kept rubbing, trying to take the effort into his upper arms, where he had strength without end. To give his right hand a rest, he pretended he had to brush the hair out of his eyes. To relieve his left, he wiped his forefinger under his nose. Then he found the proper angle. The pain in his wrists ceased and he could feel his biceps take over the task. Firmly, gently, he rubbed his palms along the knotted flesh, from just above the ankle to just below the knee, moving up, then down, to accommodate the swell of the calf.

"You can stop if you want to."

"I'm all right."

The flesh of the leg had begun to warm from the friction. To give it a chance to cool, Johnny said, "Now the other one." The calf began to unknot. Johnny continued his rubbing, but more gently now, up, down, from the ankle to just below the knee, feeling the smooth skin, the soft flesh.

"Better," Dempsey said.

"You're sure?"

She smiled. "I never lie unless it's convenient." She lifted her foot from his shoulder, moved the leg out to the side, then slowly lowered the foot onto the floor. "Thanks," she said. "You did good."

Johnny put his hands on her lap. "I think I'd better stick around."

"Why? I'm cured."

"I'm not convinced."

"Then watch." Dempsey slid sideways on the chair, got up and started walking toward her worktable at the other end of the loft, where she'd already laid out the paint tubes she expected to use that morning. With her head held high, her arms loose at her sides, she walked like a model on the runway making an exaggerated display of her wares—in this case a terrycloth bathrobe. Slowly she moved her head from side to side as if to acknowledge the spectators gaping along the runway, favoring them all with more than just a profile.

She was being stubborn; she was being dishonest. She would contradict Johnny at any cost: she would make her point no matter what degree of pain she might have to endure. Johnny would have to relent; he would have to accept Dempsey's claims of full recovery. But when he prepared himself for the exasperation he knew would come, when he'd made himself ready to accept defeat, the expected annoyance failed to arrive. Instead there had come a stab of pity that sent its ache from the bones of his toes to the back of his skull. A rush of love would weaken him, and for a moment he feared he might have a seizure. He might fall to the floor: he might writhe and twitch. He might mutter the gagged words of sorrow that he could never speak in his conscious state. But he steadied himself instead against the back of the chair where Dempsey had been sitting, took two short breaths, and said, "All right. I'm convinced." He picked up his hat from the table, gave the medal on the ribbon around his neck the obligatory brush with his sleeve, put the hat on his head, tapped it into position, straightened the visor, and flexed his knees as if to demonstrate to himself that he was capable of locomotion.

When he was leaving the loft, Dempsey was carefully and with the utmost control squeezing on to the pane of glass she used for a palette some paint, the color of which he couldn't see.

* * *

Seated in his pew, Johnny thought of the early days of his return to Dempsey, to living with her again in the loft when not at the firehouse. He had expected—in consideration of her illness—that their lovemaking would be tentative, even hesitant. Dempsey's body was unreliable, unpredictable. Anything could happen at any time. He would be easy, gentle, and careful. But Dempsey required none of it. If anything she was even more active, more challenging, more eager than in their time together those years before when she'd been perfectly well. She seemed determined that her illness not be allowed to dictate the limits of her desire, that her fervor be given full range. If the illness chose to intervene, in whatever inconvenient or sloppy manner, it would be dealt with in its own time and in its own way. Beyond that, it was to be disregarded. Anticipation of its intervention was not only discouraged, it was forbidden. Johnny had been duly instructed in the necessary protections, beginning with the condom, the strict avoidance of body fluids or discharges. If she were to bleed or throw up or have a sudden attack of diarrhea, he must not touch her until he'd donned the surgical gloves kept in ready supply at the bedside and in the bathroom. The only time the gloves became an issue was when he had scratched her neck with a toenail. It did little for their ardor that—at Dempsey's insistence—all enthusiasm ceased. The gloves were donned and a Band-Aid was applied to the scratch after it had been thoroughly irrigated and an appropriate salve rubbed into it. It took them a little while to renew their fervor, to regain their momentum, but the effort proved to be well worth it. The spectral intrusion, the reminder of death's presence in their lovemaking, made their intimacy even more precious, more passionate than before. This was their acceptance and they reveled in it with increased strength and even more tender affection. And a healthy dash of giddiness was thrown in for good measure.

Encouraged by Dempsey's undaunted participation, Johnny was able to dismiss the possibility of intrusion, the potential for interruption. But while the illness itself could be ignored when it wasn't actively present, death was never distant. If the illness could have become a deterrent, death had become quite its opposite. It was a defining force. And so, with death as an admitted participant, they had formed a workable ménage à trois, the added partner a goad to greater need, to deeper satisfactions.

Only once had the balance between them been threatened. Johnny, desperate, anguished in Dempsey's arms, had vowed that he'd protect himself no more. The condom was torn away; he'd forbid himself nothing. Nothing that Dempsey had to offer would he refuse—including death itself. All protections were to be discarded. He wanted his surrender to be total—and if that meant a surrender to death as well, the more triumphant was his determination, the more exultant his resolve.

Dempsey had settled the matter swiftly and simply. "Stop being competitive," she said, kindly but firmly. "One of us dying is enough. Put another condom on. I have no intention of getting pregnant again and I have less intention of putting myself on the pill. Here, let me. I'll do it for you." She had kissed the shaft of his penis as if placating a distraught little boy, reassuring him that he was cherished and esteemed. She slipped the condom on and said, "I know you love me. You don't have to prove it. Now come on."

And so the balance was restored, the *ménage* reinstated. None of the *trois* could presume supremacy. The old goads were reinforced: the working arrangement resubscribed.

Someone was waving at Johnny from a pew directly under the window of St. Joseph. Actually, two people were waving, one a woman, the other a little girl. The woman had taken the child's hand and was flapping it at Johnny. He recognized the woman. She had come to the firehouse to kiss his hand. This would be the child he had rescued a year and a half before, the rescue that had earned him his medal. How much the child had grown! She must be four by now.

The mother nodded at Johnny, smiling. Johnny nodded in return. The fire had been in the Bronx when he'd still been stationed there—a tenement, the flames heavily "involved" in the second and third floors. He had just been relieved by Finelli on the nozzle, and none too soon. The second alarm on his facepiece had sounded. His oxygen was out. He lowered the mask and backed down the hallway, careful not to inhale too deeply. The windows in the rooms to his left had blown out and the smoke was being pulled toward them, clearing the way in front of him.

A few steps past an axe-shattered doorway, he thought he heard a whimper. It was the rush of water through the hose snaking along the hall and up the stairs to the apartment where he'd just handed over the nozzle. He took another two steps and stopped again. He had definitely heard a whimper. Johnny went into the room and quickly took off his glove. He raised his hand to gauge the heat level, to see how hot it was closer to the ceiling. How near the fire might be. It was hot. The walls, the ceiling hadn't been opened and the fire could be there, ready to flash the room. He dropped down and began his crawl, sweeping at his sides as if he were swimming. He had less than a minute to find whoever it might be. After that, they'd both be gone. An arm is what he found first, then the skinny little body. Without even checking for a pulse or for breath, he hugged the child underneath him, against his chest, and made his crawl for the door, the child's arms and legs dragging beneath him.

At the stairs, he was able to stand up straight in the clearing smoke. Half stumbling, half falling, he made it down the one flight, tangling his feet in the hose, but managing not to trip or fall. At the landing, he placed the child on the floor. It was a girl. He tipped her head back to open the air passages and began mouth-to-mouth. But he was just giving her more smoke from his own lungs. He grabbed her up and tumbled down the next flight. At the door to the street, Tony Aponte was coming in with a halligan to open the walls. "Quick. Air. Quick!" He swung the child at him, then stumbled away to the side of the stoop, where he threw up a great black gush that included the chunks of lamb chop he'd had for dinner,

After the fire had darkened down and the smoke had vented, he went back inside to retrieve his helmet. A new one would cost one hundred and seventy-six dollars and he could think of better things to do with the money. Besides, why should he leave souvenirs behind.

He was confused about the room. After a wrong turn into a burned-out kitchen where most of the ceiling had been pulled—the refrigerator and stove were the only surviving identification—he found a room with a bed and a dresser. It had a rug on the floor and a broken window. At the baseboard of the wall to his left was his helmet.

Still coughing, he reached down to pick it up. Toward the side of the bed he saw imprinted on the rug the form of the child. There, too, on the carpet, was a stuffed animal, oval-shaped, the size of a small pillow. Through the sifted soot Johnny could see the large polka dots marking the orange back. It was a ladybug. This was the toy the child had dropped when he'd lifted her away from the floor. She had been holding on to it when he'd found her. Johnny picked it up. He'd see to it that the child got it back. The toy was soft and yielding to his touch.

Johnny slammed the helmet onto his head harder than he'd wanted to, the quick pain allowing him to make his way to the door, go through it, down the hallway, down the stairs and outside. He shoved the stuffed ladybug into the hands of a woman standing near the truck. "The kid I just brought out," he said. He did not look back nor did he look up from the street to see if he could identify the room where his helmet had been. When the lieutenant told him the child, the little girl, would be okay, he had nodded, then helped take up the hose, pulling and draining, rolling it and bedding it in the truck. He wiped a heavy string of black snot onto his sleeve. He coughed once and gave the line an extra shove to bring the whole episode to an end.

And now the child was here, the girl he'd rescued. She and her mother had come to honor him. But it was he who should honor them for coming. He would leave his pew, go to them, and thank them for being there. They warmed his heart and lifted his spirit. He must speak to them, he must touch them. He would be blessed.

Johnny stood up. As if his rising had been the expected signal the organist had been waiting for, the massive sound of the processional rumbled through the church.

The entire congregation rose to its feet, inspired by Johnny's example. The liturgy had begun. He'd have to stay where he was.

When it was time to go to Communion, the moment when Johnny would make his speech to the cardinal, he realized he'd made a mistake. He was on the wrong side of the church. When he stepped into the aisle, joining the line that approached the sanctuary for the reception of the sacrament, he noticed that he was headed toward an ordinary priest, a monsignor at best, but definitely not His Eminence. He had assumed that the cardinal would appropriate to himself the honor of offering the Eucharist to each of the firefighters, and then allow his subordinates to join him when it came time to give Communion to the other congregants. He'd assumed wrong. There at the sanctuary step was an everyday priest. What would be the point of delivering his speech to him? Johnny had prepared himself to address a Prince of the Church and now he was being shunted off to some underling—no doubt an ordained underling and a worthy one, but for Johnny's purposes, an underling nevertheless.

Johnny considered slipping across the aisle into the line of those destined to receive the host from the cardinal himself. But there, at the cardinal's left, was a man of enormous bulk, an usher obviously, but the closest thing Johnny had ever seen to a bouncer—alert to any disruption and ready to intervene in the event of any disturbances. If the man were to see Johnny change from one line to the other, he might be ready for him and hustle him away before he could get the second word out of his mouth.

But Johnny intended no desecration, no sacrilege. His reverence for the consecrated bread was beyond question. He didn't even intend to receive the Eucharist. He would simply say his speech and move on, the host untouched, the sacrament unreceived. He may have a small quarrel with some hierarchical absolutes, but his faith itself was firm. In reverence, Johnny cast his eyes down and continued his slow shuffle toward the altar. The man in front of him had a hole in the heel of his sock, showing a white circle of pale, unwrinkled skin.

Johnny was close to the sanctuary. If he was going to make his move to the other side of the aisle, it had to be now. He took another look at the priest whose ministrations he was about to refuse. The man looked like Friar Tuck in an old Robin Hood movie he'd seen on TV. His huge belly would be the envy of any Santa Claus, a promise of merriment and joviality. A second chin and a third seemed suspended from his ears, a beard not of whiskers but of flesh. His eyes bulged, expectant of wonder and delight.

The man in front of Johnny stepped forward. The priest's husky voice said the sacred words, "The Body of Christ." "Amen," the man answered. He accepted the bread and moved away. Johnny had not slipped across the aisle. After a quick glance at the cardinal, at the bouncer, he took his final step up to Friar Tuck. The priest held out the host, the thin white wafer, the bread descended from the unleavened loaves of the Passover meal. "The Body of Christ," he said. Johnny stood there. He gulped hard, then said, "Because I have to wear a condom when I'm with the woman I love, I can't marry her in the Church. If I didn't wear the condom, I'd get sick and die. She has AIDS. With the condom I can't consummate my marriage in the eyes of the Church and therefore I'm refused permission to marry."

The priest stared at him, the bulging eyes unmoving, the host still held out toward Johnny. "The Body of Christ." The priest repeated the words. Johnny took it in his hand. "Amen," he whispered. He put the bread into his mouth. From the corner of his eye he saw the bouncer stirring.

In his pew Johnny was at a complete loss as to what he should do. He had not expected to go to Communion, to actually accept the host. His life with Dempsey had placed him outside the community of the called and the chosen. Yet here he was, having just participated in the most sacred act available to anyone on this earth. He made a leftward turn of his head as if he might find knowledge and counsel in the stones of the north transept.

The cardinal was seated on the sedelia. No fewer than four priests, Friar Tuck among them, were putting away the Communion vessels, the chalices, the ciboria. Soon the time for private prayer would be over. Now His Eminence was raising his head. He would rise and the closing rites begin. Johnny had yet to say his Communion prayer. He must say it and he must say it now.

"Cure her, cure Dempsey," he blurted out. "Make her well," the words flung into the pew ahead of him. The man to his right and two men in front of him turned and looked. One of the men was the lieutenant. Johnny repeated his words, louder than before, and even more intense, as if his plea were to the men around him, that they must hear him and must answer his prayer. "Cure her. Please. Cure her." He lowered his head. The men faced front. The cardinal stood up. "Let us pray," he said.

Johnny raised his head just in time to see the mother lead the child out the great bronze door of the transept. The portal closed slowly behind them. He stared at the closed door, then at the empty place in the pew where they'd been. They were gone. And he had failed to ask for and receive their blessing.

2.

Stretched out on the wooden floor, Dempsey heard the rattling chains that told her the old freight elevator was on its way up to the loft. She closed her eyes. She'd wanted to rest a little while longer before having to tell Johnny about the latest symptoms that had sent her to the floor exhausted and twitching. The elevator chains continued rattling and clanking against the loose metal sides of the shaft, sounding more like the approach of Marley's ghost than the coming of her brave and handsome Johnny.

There, a few inches from Dempsey's nose, was the paintbrush she'd been using before the giddy rush of new symptoms had drained the energy from her entire body. The brush was one of her favorites, a red sable. She'd been using black paint—Ivory Black to be specific—and even though she knew the brush wouldn't stiffen right away—she painted with oils—it was her habit to clean the brushes almost immediately after their use. She could at least put it to soak. Or better, she should get up and get on with her work. If she were to stop, if she were to stretch herself out on the floor every time some new wave of nausea or weakness or pain racked her, she'd never get anything done. Lying there, she told herself she was being indulgent; she was being lazy; she was giving in. Not that it would alarm or even worry Johnny to see her there on the floor. She'd explained to him that whenever she got tired, she'd lie down. When she was rested, she'd get up. Rather than expend the final ounce of energy walking to the bedroom or to the couch, she'd lie down in place—and afterward simply continue to paint or do whatever she might have been doing.

More than once he'd found her exactly where she was now, at the foot of a painting, sometimes with a brush still in her hand. He'd also seen her stretched out under the long worktable, under the clutter of paint tubes, solvents, brushes, and palette knives that were the tools of her trade. She'd been known to lie down in front of the kitchen sink, or near the clothes rack that served as a closet in their bedroom, her jeans taken from the hanger crumpled up against her chest there on the floor. She had assured Johnny that she never fell or fainted. She just kept a highly accurate measure of the strength available to her, using the final expenditure to get herself safely to the floor, there to rest or sleep or relax as her condition might demand. He must never worry. If he wanted, he could check her breathing to make sure she was still alive, but beyond that, he should pass her by and allow her to rise in her own good time. She was not, she decided, ready to rise. She'd clean the brush later, giving it an extra soaking as amends for the delay.

Slowly, carefully, the elevator door screeched open and knocked against its metal casing. The inner door to the loft itself creaked on its hinges, then slowly, carefully, the elevator door screeched shut and the loft door creaked and squealed while being closed. Johnny had seen Dempsey resting and was being considerate. If he would just slam both doors open and both doors closed, the noise would be over and done in a matter of seconds. Now it was going to be prolonged. No one is noisier than someone trying to be quiet. Even with the elevator put to rest and the loft door locked, there was the drawn-out squeal of the floorboards as Johnny made his way across the room. A less thoughtful step would have squeaked the boards and gotten it over with. But now Dempsey could hear the continuing protest of the wood as the foot went slowly down, then the repeated complaint as the foot drew slowly up. She couldn't help smiling to think that if he'd just walk across the floor and forget about disturbing her, the entire ordeal would end then and there. He was finally on the rug.

Dempsey opened her eyes. Johnny had gone toward the table in the kitchen area. He'd removed his ribboned medal and was slipping down the knot of his tie. He hadn't taken off his white gloves nor the beaked pie-shaped hat that made some people mistake him for a railroad conductor. Johnny slipped off the tie and placed it on the back of a chair. His hat he put first on the arm of the couch, then, worried that it might fall, on the couch itself. He unbuttoned his jacket, slowly, slid one arm out, then the other, and hung the jacket on the back of the chair. Twice he stopped in the unbuckling of his belt, and the zipper of his fly was lowered with such measured care that it became almost erotic, a growing tension preceding a longed-for revelation.

It was when Johnny was taking off his pants that his concern was brought to an end. Standing on one foot, he'd gotten his right leg out, but when he'd put the foot onto the floor and raised the other leg, some imbalance for which he wasn't prepared forced him to hop around as if his lost equilibrium was located on one particular spot in the flooring and he was being compelled to find it assisted only by one leg and one foot. The hopping itself made little noise, although Dempsey could feel the reverberations in the floor, gentle momentary hums from the boards beneath her. But then, through some connivance of gravity and weight, a great spill of coins dropped from one of the pants pockets. Johnny accelerated the speed of his hopping. The coins, meanwhile, mostly quarters and pennies, rolled around, with one penny going back like a faithful pet to stop at Johnny's toe. A quarter made directly for Dempsey as if it had recognized in her the one true spender for which it was destined. It aimed itself at her arm and flopped onto its back only after it had touched her hand. Dempsey put her head back down on the floor.

"I woke you up," Johnny said. "I'm sorry."

"It's all right. I was awake. You were being so quiet, I couldn't stand the noise."

He grinned. In his jockey shorts, Johnny seemed skinny, almost scrawny, and being six-foot-three didn't help. He was now gathering his clothes, one piece at a time, no longer worried about being quiet—which meant he made no noise whatsoever. He headed for the bedroom, his socks padding across the floor, walking like a duck, as if he were flat-footed.

Dempsey put her head back down on the floor, hearing her hair crinkle and rasp as it rubbed against itself. She heard a drawer open in the bedroom, a door slam shut. "Someone took my last clean T-shirt."

"I wonder who."

Dempsey raised her head again. Johnny had magically located another clean T-shirt and was pulling it down over his chest. He looked fine. She had a particular fondness for the loose hang of the T-shirt, untouched by the lean stomach underneath. There was always room for her hand to slip underneath and enjoy itself in the wiry hair on his chest. Or she could anticipate a time when she might simply rest her arm across his stomach or lay her head in the hollow below the rib cage. She also liked seeing him in his socks. There was a coziness to it; he seemed more vulnerable, more comforting.

Johnny moved over to the kitchen area and picked up a dishtowel that had fallen from the back of a chair. "I'm going to make pancakes."

"Not yet. Come over here. I want company."

Johnny had taken down a mixing bowl and was staring into it as if wondering what it was for. He seemed finally to remember. He left it there on the drainboard and went to where Dempsey was lying, still stretched out on the floor. She closed her eyes again. He squatted down next to her and kissed her cheek.

"Is that you?" Dempsey asked.

"Who'd you think it was?"

Johnny stretched himself out next to her and put an arm across her side. She placed her hand over his. For a moment neither of them moved, then Johnny said, "You want to move onto the bed? The floor's kind of hard."

"No, I'm okay. Besides, even the bed's hard. Even if you floated me in the tub, it'd seem hard. So I'm okay right here. You okay here?"

"I'm okay." Johnny leaned his head closer, his nose touching a quarter nesting in her hair. He reached in and picked it out.

"Leave it," Dempsey mumbled. "You never know when I might want to make a phone call."

He left it there. They lay quietly. With his nose, Johnny brushed aside a strand of hair just below her ear and pressed his lips against her neck. Slowly he moved his nose up above her ear and ran his tongue along the rim, then gently touched it inside and flicked his tongue, but gently. After he'd brushed her neck again with the tip of his nose, he lay still, his face in her hair, the nested quarter cool against his forehead.

"I thought I was dying," Dempsey said. "Just before you got home. It felt so funny."

"Should I call the doctor?"

"No, no. Please. I'm better now. But it was like my hair started to grow and I could hear it growing. And something inside me, it sounded like Rice Krispies. Snap crackle pop. All the way through me, like I was made out of Rice Krispies and someone had just poured a bucket of milk on top of me. I thought, I'm exploding into little bits and pieces. And it tickled too. I'm dying, I said, and this is how it feels. Like Rice Krispies."

"Let me help you go lie down for a while."

"I am lying down."

"In bed I mean."

"I've got to get up and do some work. The Rice Krispies caught me right in the middle. If I'm not going to paint, I should at least clean the brushes."

"I'll clean the brushes."

She stroked his face. "No. You're not a painter. I told you. You're not allowed to clean brushes."

With Johnny's help, mostly at the elbow, she stood up. "There," she said. "See? I'm standing on my own two feet. How's that for starters?"

"I think you should lie down some more."

"I think I should go work some more. I promised Jamey."

"I think Jamey has more time than we do," Johnny said.

She turned and looked at the painting. It showed two huge men stripped to the waist, their bodies, their hands, and their faces black with coal dust, their eyes made all the more fierce and glaring by the grime surrounding them. One was heaving a great shovelful of coal into the circular maw of a furnace. The other was bending down, his back a huge hump of muscle, his shovel pushed into a mound of coal just to the side of the furnace door. The light from the fire made the coal glisten, flickering against it, anticipating the true fire soon to come. The fire itself was orange and gold, not so much pointed flames as one mass of contending colors devouring each other, replenishing each other, making sure that their struggle would never end. Caught in the furnace's flare, the men's bodies shone like polished wood: the forehead, the upper arm, the chest of the man closest to the furnace door, the humped back, the left cheek and ear, the entire left arm of the man shoveling into the mound of coal. The men seemed to work with a malevolence equal to the malevolence of the fire itself. They seemed calmly maddened by the task, determined to excite the flames to an even greater devastation. This was her painting *The Burial of Lazarus*. Lazarus's body, Dempsey claimed, was already inside, and it seemed that the two men were making sure that it would never be raised, would never be called forth and given life again.

Johnny had at first complained about the inaccuracy of the painting. Lazarus had been buried in a tomb inside a cave with a stone blocking the entrance. He had not been cremated. Dempsey explained that this was her painting and she could bury him any way she wanted to bury him. Johnny's real objection, of course, had more to do with her own burial than with the burial of Lazarus. In her will she had directed that her friend Winnie, the executor, cremate her and toss her ashes from the Brooklyn Bridge. Johnny told her this was a rejection of her body. She was punishing it, getting even for what it was doing to her. He, she said, was exactly right. And went right on painting, stoking the fire.

It was the paintings, of course, that had brought Dempsey and Johnny together again after their separation. The idea for a series of Lazarus paintings, as she had already explained, had come to Dempsey from her friend Jamey, who was dying at the time. When he had been diagnosed with AIDS, he had planned a series he would have painted: *Lazarus Afflicted*, *Lazarus Being Cared for by His Sisters*, *The Burial of Lazarus*, and finally, *The Raising of Lazarus*. (The death itself he wanted to omit; he wasn't ready for so immediate a confrontation.)

When Jamey had gotten too sick to do the work himself, Dempsey said she would do the paintings and Jamey could pose. Jamey agreed and moved into Dempsey's loft, but then he became too sick even to pose. He died before she'd even begun.

The project then became Jamey's memorial. His dying, she had to admit, had not been an easy time for either of them. He had developed the habit of complaining, as if it were one more syndrome of the virus. This had not been Jamey's style, but for the final weeks of his life he had become what Dempsey preferred to call "testy." The truth was that he had become a chronic complainer. Nothing was right. Nothing she did for him was acceptable. Not her care, not her cooking, not her cleaning. Most of all her cleaning. If she cleaned, she was deliberately disturbing him; if she didn't clean, she was endangering his health by allowing dust to gather and the virus to proliferate.

When, at the very end, she'd had to feed him—even spoon in water, which he could no longer draw up through a straw—he was infuriated by her ineptitude. Even though she had learned from Winnie, who'd done similar duty for her friend Caitlin, to feed from the tip of the spoon, not from the side, some dribble would invariably fall onto his chin, neck, chest, or bathrobe. It was, Dempsey told him, because he bit the spoon. He should just let her do the work. Then there'd be a quarrel, with Jamey falling out of bed—actually Dempsey's bed, which she'd surrendered to him for the duration.

It was while she was struggling to get him up off the floor, back into the bed and straightening out the pillows under his head that they would reconcile. This had become the pattern: they would fight, yell—even, on Jamey's better days, throw things—until Jamey either collapsed or had a coughing fit or, once, a convulsion. Then, during the frantic efforts to help him, to undo the damage, they would both apologize, both beg forgiveness and sometimes weep. There would be a brief respite from Jamey's whining until Dempsey's next ministration, which per usual, would be insufficient, inept or attempted murder.

This had not been Jamey's way. Before the illness, he'd been cheerful, agreeable, accommodating, and affectionate. Which was why Dempsey had offered to take him in. She'd liked his company. He liked hers. He would die in a state of mutual regard. It hadn't happened that way.

Jamey's last words to his friend—aspirated and barely audible, but still a snarl—were: "Never mind. Forget it."

She'd been trying to lift his hips so she could slide a fresh diaper into place before he soiled the sheets. He hadn't seemed that heavy but by now had become dead weight, a gathered center of gravity already responding to some primal pull back to the earth. When she'd rolled him toward her to begin to place the diaper, a spill of yellow fluid came from his mouth, onto his pillow, smelling like rotted vanilla pudding. She'd quickly righted him again, then realized he might choke on whatever it was he'd been trying to disgorge. She rolled him toward her again. No more fluid came. Jamey jerked his head away from her as if she'd been trying to rub his nose in the mess he'd made. And so he died, his bowels emptying themselves in a swift leakage escaping onto the flowered sheet—huge daisies—that Jamey had brought with him when he'd first moved in.

Dempsey was unable to convince herself that the real Jamey was being revealed in his final weeks and days. Jamey had become petty, whiny, surly, and snarling, without even the good grace to be merely sullen. This was the revealed Jamey. The previous Jamey, Dempsey felt, had been a construct, manufactured from bits and shards of charm, wit, and warmth. No wonder he was such a popular artist. His paintings, then his collages, were obviously the product of an experienced manipulator. The effort he had expended in the creation of himself—with such notable success—was easily transferred to the canvas, the fabric, the wood, whatever medium he might choose. The mean-spirited, sneering, whining Jamey could have created next to nothing. It would have been crabbed, petulant, like the work of some she could name. But he had invested what spirit he'd been given in creating a workable image of himself, one that could project itself into art that was both skillful and pleasing.

But then, on a winter afternoon, not long before Jamey had died on the last day of February, Dempsey realized she had been wrong. A wet snow was falling outside.

She had turned on the lamp near the couch and the bulb over the kitchen sink so the loft would have pools of warm light, the color of burnished leather, not the glare of the spots she used for her paintings. She'd lit the bedside lamp as well, tipping the shade away so the glare would fall lightly into the room. Jamey's temperature was one hundred and four and Dempsey was moving a cool washcloth over his face—slowly, gently, to soothe the fevered forehead, the cheeks, the dehydrated lips. Slowly, slowly she let the washcloth be drawn across his closed eyes, across his mouth, then along his neck, under his chin. It was while the cloth was passing under the chin that Jamey raised his head higher so the cloth could pass more easily. Never had Dempsey been gentler, more measured in her movement than she was then. As the cloth continued its near-glacial move, Jamey opened his eyes. From his mouth, from his chest, came a sigh of such deep contentment that Dempsey, without effort, became even gentler, more measured. The sigh came again and Dempsey saw in Jamey's eyes a look of sorrowing gratitude that, in its sweetness, seemed close to an ultimate fulfillment. The eyes closed again and Dempsey dipped the washcloth into the basin, wrung it out, and began the slow move across the forehead.

With quick jerks from side to side, Jamey refused the cloth. "Why can't I ever be left alone!" His voice was abrupt and had more energy than Dempsey had heard for a week. She dropped the cloth into the basin, letting a few drops splash onto Jamey's cheek. He hissed, then clutched the sheet into his fists and held it tight.

He had become again the familiar ingrate, but it was too late. Dempsey had seen for just that one moment the real Jamey and nothing would ever take from her the truth of what she'd seen. Standing at a window, contemplating the peaceful snow, she realized this meanness had been inflicted on him, yet another opportunistic infection—like the pneumocystic pneumonia, the cytomegalovirus that preyed upon his exhausted immunities. Jamey was not mean; he *had* meanness. Meanness was his illness, not himself. Jamey was not spiteful, he *had* spite. Jamey was not ungrateful; he *had* ingratitude.

People do not become cancer; they do not become tuberculosis. They have cancer and they die of it; they have tuberculosis and it kills them. Jamey had meanness and it was going to kill him. But at least Dempsey was now in possession of this distinction. Her affectionate, charming, warmhearted friend had been momentarily returned to her. Now she could forget his terminal petulance and recognize it for what it was—a malignity that had taken hold of her kind and gifted friend. It would bring him, sneering and whining, to his death.

The pancake batter was ready. Dempsey watched Johnny put the first two spoonfuls onto the griddle. The batter rose and began sputtering around the edges. The smell that only pancakes can produce, more welcoming even than bread, began to overwhelm the smell of paint and turpentine that usually took over the loft. Bubbles began popping open on the surface of the batter. Johnny flipped the pancakes over. They were crisply ridged, with a darkening brown in the middle. As Dempsey watched, they puffed up higher, then settled down. Johnny slipped a corner of the spatula under the surface and lifted the edge to see if the pancake was done. He then slid the spatula under each in turn, stacking one on top of the other, and slipped them onto the plate in front of her. He shoved the syrup and the butter closer, an encouragement rather than a needed assistance. Dempsey's reach could have found them easily enough, but Johnny obviously wanted to make an offering, a small act of caring and of love.

Just as Dempsey was about to pour the syrup over the pancakes, she heard the chirping sound of her pill dispenser. Without letting the flow of syrup continue to its natural conclusion, she set the jug down, wiped her fingers on her napkin and pulled the dispenser out of her jeans pocket. Shaped like a cosmetic compact, the dispenser held all the pills prescribed for the day. The beeper had been set to remind her that the appointed time had come.

Once more the chirping sounded. Dempsey shut off the beeper with a single swift click of her thumb. Using her thumb, she popped it open and delicately took out a tiny burgundy-and-yellow capsule, which she immediately deposited into the gallon-sized brandy snifter that seemed to be the centerpiece of the table.

Inside the snifter was a mound of pills that looked like beach glass—blues, purples, yellows, with a scattering of maroons and a few reds, but with too many whites, grays, and tans to make the collection as interesting as she'd like.

This was Dempsey's medicine depository. AZT thrown in with Zovirax and Diflucan, old bits of Bactrim and Rimactane pressed against Propulsid, Selenium, and Pyrazinamide. There was even some Senokot and a full bottle of vitamin C thrown in for color.

For the past month and a half, it had been Dempsey's habit, when it came time to take her medicine, to faithfully remove each pill or capsule from her dispenser and toss it into the snifter. Only at assigned times would this be done; no contribution was postponed, none was anticipated before its prescribed moment. Never had she been tempted to simply empty a new prescription fresh from the pharmacy into the snifter all at once and be done with it. Instructions were to be followed, the schedule faithfully adhered to. With her, or within hearing distance, at all times was her dispenser with its birdlike beeper, reminding her it was time to make a deposit into the snifter.

If she was out of the loft, at the store, in the street, on

a bus or the subway, wherever—the beeper was obeyed absolutely and without pause. The capsule whose time had come was removed from the dispenser carefully, respectfully—as if she were selecting an enticing tidbit from among a generous offering. It was put into a pocket, its removal from the company of its peers, an immutable indication that it would be deposited at the first opportunity into the out-sized brandy snifter. Back in the loft, before she did anything else—even take off her coat or go to the bathroom—the medicines whose time had come and gone would be sprinkled down into the growing collection with the same elegant gesture Dempsey might use to add a few more croutons to a salad.

Like any serious collector, she found great satisfaction in the growth of her hoard. When enough pills and capsules had been pitched into the snifter to cover the bottom, her sense of accomplishment brought a fond smile to her face. When enough had accumulated to create a small mound, she knew she was on her way to a notable achievement.

For Doctor Norstar she provided a welcome relief from those patients who often balked at an increase in their medication. Instead of groans or frightened concern about added intrusions into her system, Dempsey now greeted a changed or enhanced menu with eagerness and gratitude. When Doctor Norstar would patiently present her reasonings, taking time to explain the difference between pharmacokinetic interactions and pharmacodynamic interactions, Dempsey would nod her understanding. But her eagerness, her hope, was founded on a wish that this latest attempt to delay her doom would come in red or at least green, a contribution that would enliven a collection that threatened to be overwhelmed by the beige, the buff, and most boring of all, just plain medicinal white. (She knew that white was the presence of all colors, but she preferred to have the inclusions broken down into more exciting components.)

Dempsey had started her collection the day she'd thrown up on a sculpture by her friend Harden Lavrans in a gallery on Greene Street. She didn't particularly care for the sculpture, a pyramid of black spheres that resembled—no, replicated exactly—some cannonballs she'd seen any number of times placed in pyramids next to Civil War cannons in any number of town memorials. Knowing Harden, however, and his work, she knew that this was more than a pile of cannonballs. They could be basketballs, and being black, they suggested both black sexuality and masculinity as well as commentary on the success of black male ascendancy: sports. Then, too, the structure was an added commentary on the subject. It was a pyramid. Slaves had built the pyramids. By extension, blacks had made possible one of the wonders of the world. The contrast between pyramid building and playing basketball was intended as a topic for meditation, with special consideration given to the fact that only one would rise to the top. The others no more than support, needfully suppressed. But then, at the same time, these were replicated cannonballs. This might suggest, for those perceptive enough to see, that blacks were considered cannon fodder. Or bombs, ready to explode.

Dempsey had sighed. Harden was a tow-headed Scandinavian from Iowa—and about twenty years behind the times. In the Sixties, full appreciation would have been given to his true but obvious statement. Critics would have fallen all over themselves in congratulation for having seen what Dempsey was seeing now. They would have beamed at having solved the puzzle, for decoding the intellectual messages hidden within, for ferreting out the political agenda, for being challenged, in their reviews, to demonstrate their acuity, their unfailing and necessary ability to make a great deal out of very little. Dempsey herself had, within seconds, experienced all this and was probably well on her way to extracting more from the quite scrutable sculpture, but she'd thrown up instead.

She had not intended so harsh a criticism. What disturbed her most was the content and color of her vomit. Instead of the rejected remains of a decent meal, there, for all to see, unchanged in form or substance, were the pills she'd taken hastily, just before entering: Zovirax, Myambutol, Rimactane, Pyridoxine. Some of the pills slipped down into the crevices between the balls, others seemed stuck where they'd landed and the rest slowly slid along the slope of the balls so they dripped onto the floor.

With two quick breaths, Dempsey recovered from the spasm of throwing up and, as if she had simply deposited a cleansing agent onto the sculpture, knelt down and proceeded to wipe and rub her scarf along the balls, gathering up her pills and soaking up her mucous into the woolen cloth. The young man attending the gallery was at his desk in an alcove and the one other visitor was at the window looking out over Greene Street or, perhaps, at another exhibit across the way. Just as she was picking up a Zovirax—a beautiful robin's-egg-blue capsule—the attendant came out from the alcove. Passing by as he went toward the man at the window, he said somewhat cheerfully, "It's probably a good idea not to touch the artwork."

Dempsey let the Zovirax lie where it lay, hoping some unsuspecting mouse wouldn't mistake it for an interesting morsel and give itself the hallucinations mentioned among the several possible side effects.

By the time she had rolled up the contaminated scarf, she had vowed never to take another pill, another capsule, another dose of anything prescribed. If that's what they all looked like inside of her, no wonder she felt lousy. And besides, what if she had come to the opening of the show and this had happened then—in a room crowded with people more than several of whom could, after one quick glance at the undigested meds, give a complete and accurate diagnosis of her illness, her condition, and possibly her prognosis. This was knowledge she was not yet prepared to divulge to the public at large. The pain and pleasure the knowledge of her illness might cause would have to wait until the day when she could no longer conceal her condition or, more likely, until she had decided that she herself was ready to inflict the pain and pleasure the revelation would create. It would not be a public spectacle as it might have been just now. She may have little or no control over the epidemic; all the more reason to keep control over the announcement of its presence.

From now on—she was jamming the scarf ends into her tote bag, punishing them for popping out twice now—if her body wanted to disintegrate and die, that would be its business. It was free either to oppose or to cooperate with the virus to which she had introduced it when she was still on drugs. No more prodding and prompting from her and from Doctor Norstar.

The idea had an extravagance that appealed to her, a stubbornness of which she heartily approved, a sense of vengeance that gratified her need for spite, for contempt. Of course, a time of testing would come. Would she be willing to accept the fevers and sweats, the diarrhea, the hiccups, the chest pains and headaches that would assault her at will when a simple popped pill held the promise of relief? Could she ignore the weight loss, the distended belly, the swollen legs and ankles? Would she be able to sustain herself through periods of feeling just plain awful—as if no particular part of her anatomy was being attacked but, instead, the illness had invaded her entire being, targeting not just her body but her spirit, a dull meanness, an abusive discontent, an exhausted disgust with all the separate components that defined her being, each contending with the other as to which would be attacked next?

Doctor Norstar, of course, would be a problem. When told she'd need no more medicine, the doctor wouldn't argue; she'd just become exasperated. This, more than any prospect of pain, prompted Dempsey to reconsider. Doctor Norstar's regard had been, perhaps, more sustaining than the medicines she had dispensed. For Dempsey to reject her ministrations, to invite her disdain, would be impossible. There was nothing Dempsey wouldn't do for Doctor Norstar. When the doctor had told her to eat Jell-O, she'd eaten Jell-O. When it was no more than suggested that Dempsey might walk a mile a day, Dempsey walked twice that, down to Battery Park and back. When it rained, she'd walk back and forth in the loft like a swimmer doing laps. When Doctor Norstar told her to make sure the loft was properly ventilated, Dempsey finally—after three years of procrastination—installed not one but two vents. If Doctor Norstar were to tell her to swim the Hellespont, she would at least give it a try. And if Doctor Norstar gave her a prescription, she would, without question, accept it and follow the instructions faithfully.

Deceit suggested itself. Dempsey, ever eager to have her own way without jeopardizing approval, almost immediately decided she'd simply lie (by omission) to

Doctor Norstar. She'd take the prescriptions, have them filled, then collect the contents in the large brandy snifter she'd once used for a terrarium. Dempsey would see, hour by hour, day by day, the toxic, nauseating medicines rise: she would observe what she had spared her already weakened system. Pleased that she had devised a plan that involved stubbornness, deceit, and the kind of self-dramatization she particularly enjoyed, Dempsey gave the top of Harden's sculpture one more brush with her hand to collect and absorb any particles of the virus that might still be clinging for dear life to the surface she'd so recently polished with her heavings.

Dempsey went to the counter that separated the alcove from the gallery and began signing her name in the register. She wanted Harden to know she'd come. The smell of vomit reached her nostrils; she hoped it came from the scarf in her tote, or even her breath, and not from the sculpture she'd just defiled. After jamming the scarf deeper down, she began adding her last name to her first, but before she could finish—between the *o* and the *a* of *Coates*—one further thought came to her. Calvin, an actor friend, had gone blind. Cynthia, an illustrator of children's books, had gone mad. Retinitis for Calvin, dementia for Cynthia. Would she, Dempsey, refuse, in her resolve, protection against these final afflictions? She wrote the *a* in her name, then stopped again. Would she be willing, without a fight, to surrender her mind and her sight? If she could agree to this, would it indicate that dementia had already begun? A painter to sacrifice her eyes; an artist to dismiss her mind?

The pen hovered over the page. It seemed for a moment that she would cross out what she'd already written. The pen wavered just above the *a*, then was almost slammed down onto the paper. Pressing firmly into the page, she completed her name, *Dempsey Coates,* and let the pen drop onto the counter next to the book. With her name, her very own sacred name, she had subscribed to all that she had thought. The pact was made, immutable and beyond revision. She would prove herself greater than her illness; there would be nothing it could inflict that she would not endure. The triumph would be hers. If, that is, she could stick to her guns. Even though they were aimed directly at herself.

Dempsey now added another pill to the snifter, this one a fine strong red. She then snapped the lid shut, reset the timer, and put the dispenser back into her pocket.

"Maybe you should start taking your pills again," Johnny said. "I mean, since you felt so funny this morning, like something was really happening."

"No thank you."

"Maybe this is something new starting. It could get worse."

"That's all right. I kind of liked it. Snap. Crackle. Beats pneumonia—although it's probably not half the fun dementia's going to be."

She picked up the syrup and continued to pour it over the pancakes. "Look," she said. "See how beautiful it is? The color, the way it pours, the way it spreads over the pancakes and falls down the sides. And then we get to eat it. What could be better?"

"A pill."

Dempsey set the syrup down and slowly drew her hand away, delicately, in tribute to the syrup's beauty. She even rubbed the tips of her fingers together to catch the feel of whatever might have stuck. "Then take a pill," she said. "Help yourself."

"You want me to? I will."

"Go ahead."

"If you won't take them, I will. How about that?"

"Your funeral, not mine."

"Good."

She watched him put down his fork and stare at the pancakes on his plate. "Don't, Johnny. Almost any of them could kill you," she said. And you need to live." She picked out a burgundy-and-yellow capsule. "Rimactane," she said. "Wrecks your liver. It also makes you shit and piss orange." She dropped it back into the snifter and stirred a finger in among the pills. "It's all here. Seizures? Nausea? Bone damage? Take your pick. And that's just for starters." She fished out the robin's-egg blue. "Zovirax. Hallucinations. Or here's one I suppose I should take myself, Isoniazid. You might see bright colors, strange designs."

Johnny picked up his fork and pushed his pancakes from one side of his plate to the other. "They help more than they hurt," he muttered. He dipped his hand in. "Then I'll take a red one." He took one out and popped it into his mouth.

"No, definitely not that one. Please, Johnny. Not that one."

Johnny picked the pill off his tongue. "Why not?"

"Just not that one."

He waited, then asked, "Is it one of those?"

"Just don't swallow it."

"Is it? Is it one of those? One of the ones Winnie gave you?"

"Oh, them. No. I never should have told you about them."

"She shouldn't have given them to you."

"Oh? And what's the alternative? That I starve to death while my body bloats like a Macy's balloon? That my hair drops out of my head and my insides, my stomach, my liver, my kidneys give out?"

Johnny said nothing.

"And then, at last! Dementia to the rescue! Is that what you want?"

"No," he said quietly. "It's not what I want."

Dempsey looked at him a moment, then said, "Maybe I'm crazy already. Maybe it isn't anything physical that happens to the brain that drives us mad at the end. Maybe it's the epidemic itself, our knowing what's happening, what's going to happen. Maybe that's enough to send us over the edge. Maybe this is the beginning and pretty soon it will be finished."

She leaned her head back as far as it could go and blinked at the ceiling. "When I'm crazy," she said, "maybe that's when I'll know what to do for the raising of poor Lazarus. When the dementia finally hits me, that's when I'll be able to paint the poor man's Resurrection. Maybe only someone crazy would really know. So I've got to keep myself alive until then, until I go mad. It's there—the painting. I know it is. But my brain's got to get itself really rattled first, really stirred up. Then it'll come. Lazarus, rising, shooting up and out of my crazed brain and splattering himself all over the inside of my skull. Maybe I'll be blind by then. I'll be blind and crazy and then I'll see it: *The Raising of Lazarus*. And I'll paint it just like that, just the way it really is. It doesn't matter I'm blind. It doesn't matter I'm crazy. I'll paint it. And it'll be right."

Lightly she touched Johnny's hand. "Keep me alive until then," she said quietly. "That's all I ask. Keep me going. Save me for the dementia. It can happen. It happens all the time, a lot more than it used to. All the medicines, they keep you alive so you can finally go crazy." She smiled a wan smile. "Tell me you'll keep me alive until then. Promise?"

"And you promise me you won't take the pills Winnie gave you?"

Dempsey leaned back in her chair, still smiling but sadder now. "Did I tell you you're the handsomest man who has ever sat at this table? And as for that pill you've got, go ahead and swallow. It's Zithromax. But be forewarned it'll make your vagina itch."

"Please," said Johnny. "Promise."

Again she gently touched the back of his hand. "As a matter of fact, you're the handsomest, the most beautiful man who has ever stopped out of that noisy elevator." She paused, then added, "And you can cook too. How about that?"

Johnny raised his hand, lifting hers to his lips. Gently, sadly, he kissed it, looked at it a moment, then, more slowly, kissed it again.

3.

Johnny had heard that using newspaper was best for cleaning windows—something about the newsprint giving the glass a higher shine. But since newsprint had been superseded and he'd never liked the print smearing onto his hands, he always used paper towels—a luxury, a waste, but so what? The credit he'd accrued just by washing the windows more than compensated for the needless extravagance.

More often than not, the symbiosis between Johnny and his conscience worked effectively to the benefit of his ease and the enhancement of his self-regard. His free will was allowed to remain fairly free, permitting him to go after what he wanted without too much reflective foot dragging. All of which means that Johnny was washing the third-floor windows of the firehouse, inside and out, using paper towels, and enjoying himself.

Why Johnny had chosen this particular day to wash windows was beyond his understanding. It was hot; it was humid. The ailanthus trees in the small area between the firehouse and the brick wall of the warehouse behind gave him some cover, the leaves brushing against his back, his head, his arm, or waving slowly above him, fanning his neck, cooling the perspiration trickling down from under his hair. But the stones and bricks had been baking steadily for over a week, pulling in the heat. They were now in their sated state, warming the air to oven temperatures best suited for a turkey, a pork loin, or even a pizza. Still, Johnny had found himself missing the view, the lemon green of the ailanthus leaves, the grime-encrusted bricks, and the bright, clean gleam of the glass itself. And so he'd set to work, heat or no heat, the ailanthus leaves tickling his hair, his neck, and, if he was lucky, the inside of his ear.

His legs clamped over the windowsill, he rubbed the bunched towel against the outside glass, clearing away the dried cleaning wax he himself had bought so the job would be properly done. (Liquid sprays left an uneven gloss.) With his index finger inside the towel, he traced along the edges, digging into the corners, to make sure no smudges remained. To be sloppy about washing a window was a contradiction. It made the entire operation useless. It would blight the vision he was determined to make clear.

These were his favorite moments in the whole procedure: sitting outside, looking into the room through the clean window. The separation provided by the glass, the changed, opposing point of view, gave the inside of the room a strange and pleasing presence. What had been so familiar, the furniture and the artifacts among which he himself had moved with such easy inattention, now became remote. The lockers, wooden cupboards actually, that lined the walls, the lumpy couch, the overstuffed chair, the smudged television set arranged at the far end of the room, the old rowing machine the men themselves had bought to help fight off the flesh so easily accumulated during the inaction between alarms and excursions—all these became objects of fascination. Even Rickey Cameron there by his locker, rolling some socks and throwing them onto a shelf, had become a stranger, removed. Ed Acosta, pulling away at the oars of the rowing machine, appeared like someone who did not know him, whose life did not include Johnny Donegan.

What Johnny was being given was a glimpse of his absence, the world familiar but without him. This is how it would look when he was gone. He was being given a vision of a continuing action in which he would have no part. The vision he accepted as a gift, grateful that he'd been offered a sight so rare, pleased that he'd been allowed to observe, to participate in this strange moment of his own nonexistence.

Johnny pulled himself back from the window and looked for any remaining traces of the dried wax. He knew that Noonan and Rigney would come looking, determined to spot some missed streaks or clouded patches. Noonan would be stern; Rigney gleeful if an imperfection could be found. Noonan would pretend grave disappointment at the failure; Rigney would expect Johnny to revise his pretensions to adequacy.

Just as he was about to raise the window and climb back inside he saw a man coming up the stairs, into the room. It was the priest, the Friar Tuck who'd given him Communion at the cathedral. What Johnny first saw was the enormous face rising by degrees up out of the stairwell, the balding head, the black suit worn to a silken shine, the great shoulders, then the huge torso, lifted step by step up into the room. A measured pace gave dignity to the man's arrival, a stateliness, a cadence and rhythm not necessarily imposed by the steps themselves. He was giving the handrail only the lightest touch with his fingertips, an acknowledgment rather than an employment. The one concession to gravitational pull was the downward bend of the shoulders, the forward thrust of the head. Perhaps the man was so accustomed to listening—to hearing confessions, to being heaped with insoluble problems—that his head was permanently inclined, prepared to be burdened by whatever ghastly or dreary difficulty a penitent might want to unload. He had long given up trying to right himself, to straighten his shoulders, to lift his head, to withdraw from the posture his calling had laid upon him.

Perhaps his calling accounted as well for the bulging eyes. To Johnny it seemed not impossible that the man had been told some gigantic truth that he was still struggling to comprehend, a truth so shattering that the eyes had opened wider to receive it and had never been able to return to their former repose.

Cameron and Acosta didn't exactly jump to attention but they did manage to perform some respectful equivalent. Acosta swung around on the seat of the rowing machine. Cameron stopped tossing his socks into his locker, as if it were an act too frivolous to be performed in the presence of a priest. Acosta stood up next to the rowing machine as if ready for inspection.

The priest nodded to the two men. Cameron shook his hand, then Acosta. Now all three of them were looking toward Johnny, Cameron pointing and Acosta bobbing his head in Johnny's direction. The priest nodded. Johnny was the man he'd come to see.

Acosta and Cameron, without being asked, prepared to leave the room. Acosta placed the oars neatly into position and rubbed his hand across the seat of the rowing machine. Cameron snapped the padlock on his locker, but so quietly that Johnny heard nothing through the glass. Acosta backed out of the room, waiting until he was at the top of the stairs before showing the least concern about where he was headed. Cameron shook the priest's hand again, then gave a light tap to his locker door as he passed, a signal that the door was not to reopen in his absence.

The priest turned again toward Johnny. Johnny raised a hand then pointed to the window glass in front of him. He held up the bunched paper towel and made circular motions in the air. The priest nodded again in understanding and Johnny accepted the nod as permission to continue. Pretending to have seen a smudge, he rubbed the towel vigorously in the upper left corner, squinted, rubbed again, then took a few seconds to check for further failure. He found none.

The priest watched, patient, unmoving.

Up went the window and Johnny slid himself into the room. His joints—ankle, knee, and hip—were stiff and he quickly lifted one leg, then the other, to reassure them that their ordeal was over. "Sorry, Father," he said, "I just had that little bit to finish."

The priest held out his hand. "Father Dunphy. You may remember me. I'm sorry to interrupt." He spoke in soft tones as if to an acquaintance of long standing for whom he felt a quiet sympathy. What surprised Johnny was that the man was not perspiring. No sweat showed on his forehead or on his face. His black suit was unrumpled; there were no stains or blotches anywhere, not even under the arms. Nor were there any markings on the starched Roman collar. The man was obviously exempt from discomfort.

"I remember you," Johnny said. "From the Sunday at the cathedral."

"And you're John Donegan. A Mr. Conboy helped me find you. He—Mr. Conboy—is in your headquarters. In Brooklyn. Because of your medal. He showed me the Medal Day books for the past three years. There you were. A little over a year ago—you rescued a little girl."

"Right."

"Your hair isn't as red as I remember it."

"It changes. It's really more brown or blond. Sometimes. Depending."

"And you're taller."

Johnny shrugged. Father Dunphy continued to look directly at him, the quiet voice contradicting the bulging eyes.

"And you have to use a condom so you won't get sick and die."

Johnny looked at the crumpled toweling in his hand. "Yeah." He shifted the towel from his right hand to his left, then bunched it even more.

"You love her."

"Yes. I mean yes, Father." He loosened his grip on the towel and pitched it toward the wastebasket near the lockers. It bounced off the rim and landed, after a tipsy roll, at the foot of Cameron's cot. He made a move to retrieve it, but stopped himself.

"You may try again if you like," the priest said.

"It doesn't matter." When the priest said nothing, Johnny went over and picked up the wadded paper, went back to where he'd been and took aim. Instead of making the toss, however, he lowered his hand, went to the wastebasket and dropped it in. It lay in between some of the other toweling he'd already discarded and a stray single brown sock thrown there by Cameron. He considered staying there, near the lockers, but when Father Dunphy didn't turn toward him, he returned to where he'd been. Perhaps he had to be there, in that one spot, for the priest to speak to him.

After Johnny had placed his feet in their previous position and resumed as much of his pose as was possible without the crumpled towel to occupy his hands, the priest said, "I am here in obedience to my bishop, the cardinal. It would seem that the usher to my left reported your statement to one of the assistant priests in the Chancery. The assistant priest found an occasion on which to mention it to His Eminence. I myself am not assigned to the Chancery. Or to the cathedral. I was chosen to assist His Eminence that day because one of my parishioners, a firefighter, Joseph Bolles, was killed in the line of duty last fall. You may remember."

"I remember. I was outside the church, in the ranks. Greenwich Village, right?"

Father Dunphy nodded. "In any event, I was sent for by His Eminence. He asked for verification of what you'd said. About the condoms. I verified it. He asked for verification—a second time—that I offered you the sacred host. I verified that too. There is a concern that you may have received the sacrament unworthily, that I am culpable, and that, if this is true, I must repent and you must do the same."

"I hadn't intended to go to Communion. To receive, to accept the host. I only wanted to say what I said and let it go at that. But I didn't intend to say it to you. I wanted to say it to the cardinal. And then walk away, without having gone to Communion."

"Then I should not have encouraged you to receive the sacrament."

"Then why did you?"

"You looked so—so needful. I felt that you—you of all the men there were most in need of God's presence, of the Body of Christ."

He was looking directly at Johnny, his voice low, his gaze calm, with a sad perplexity. Johnny looked down at the floor, then turned his head toward the windows he'd been cleaning. "I was mad. I mean, I was angry is all. At the cardinal."

"Ah yes. Condoms."

"I want to get married, Father. But I can't. My pastor on Staten Island, Father Tyson, he said we couldn't. He said he checked with the cardinal's office—the Chancery is it—and the cardinal or someone there, he said it wasn't possible."

Father Dunphy fingered the second button on his jacket, rubbing it as if it were a talisman that would give him some hint as to what he should do next. Apparently the button told him to sit down on the side of the rowing machine and stare at his shoes. When the button had completed its message and he had complied, he put his hand on his knee and simply sat there.

"Can I get you something, Father? Something cold—you know—to drink?"

The priest thought a moment, then nodded. He also managed to smile, but without dismissing the sad perplexity from his face. "Yes, you can get me something."

"What? A Pepsi? What?"

"The gift of Solomon, the one he asked for when God told him he could have whatever he wanted. An understanding heart." The smile widened, the perplexity, the sadness still there. "That's what Solomon asked for. Of all the things, in all the world, an understanding heart. Not a bad answer, huh?"

"There's a Coke machine down in the kitchen." When Father Dunphy made no reply, he added, "But there are other drinks. Ginger ale. Root beer. Orange, I think. And grape. It'd be cold."

"This woman you want to marry, she has AIDS."

"Yes."

"That's why the condom."

"Yes."

"And that's why you can't marry."

"Right. Because if I always use a condom, the marriage isn't consummated. It wouldn't be valid; it wouldn't be a real marriage until I—well—until I didn't use a condom. And Dempsey—she won't let me without one."

"Dempsey is the woman?"

"Dempsey is the woman."

"And she's worried you might get AIDS."

"She says because she's afraid of getting pregnant but I know it's to protect me."

"Father Tyson, you know, is right—about the marriage."

"I guess so."

"He explained that the marriage isn't fulfilled, isn't completed until—until the sex act is performed without impediment."

"Yeah. He explained it. In almost those exact same words."

"Sorry. We do resort to formulae from time to time."

Johnny squatted down on his haunches in front of the priest. "But he's wrong. I know he's wrong."

"Oh? I'm sure two millennia of theologians will be interested to hear your reasoning."

"I don't use a condom to thwart the marriage. I do it so I won't get sick and die. And I told him—Father Tyson—there's got to be such a thing as first intent. And my first intent, my only intent is not to get AIDS. What am I supposed to do? Consummate the marriage and then die?"

"In a word, yes."

"But that's stupid. It's wrong. It has to be wrong."

"Please. Don't make me go into what constitutes a valid marriage. You'd either get bored or you'd get angry all over again. So what's the point?"

"The point is that I want to get married. I love her. And I want to marry her. And there's a practical side to it. If she's my wife, when she gets really sick later on—when it gets close to—you know—to the end—to when she's—she's dying, I can get official leave and be with her all the time. This way, I'm going to have to quit my job, except I'm going to have to lie to her and tell her it's a leave of absence. I have to marry her. Why can't anyone understand that?"

"It's not a matter of understanding."

"All right, then. I won't use a condom. I'll 'consummate' the marriage. And if I get sick, I get sick. It's a chance I'll take. Except she won't let me. I know she won't let me.

And I can't lie to her, for obvious reasons. And what if she does get pregnant? What do we do then?"

"How can I possibly know?"

"I'll tell you what we do. She dies, the child dies, I die. Hooray, hooray. Good Catholic deaths. A happy death, I think it's called. We can even get the last rites. Hooray all over again. Hooray for me, hooray for Dempsey, hooray for the kid. Especially the kid. At least it didn't die a bastard, poor bastard."

"And what would you like me to do?"

"Marry us. That's all. Marry us."

"But it wouldn't —"

"It would! Before God I swear to you, it would be a true and real and honest and valid and consummated and all those other words marriage."

"If you need the legality of a marriage, if she becomes Mrs. Donegan and she gets the insurance and you get the leave of absence, then why not just go down to City Hall? For all these legalities, that would be enough."

Johnny got up. "But it wouldn't be a true marriage. I'm a Catholic. City Hall doesn't do it for me. If I'm not married by a priest, I'm not married. And I'm not going to fake it."

"You realize, of course, that you're being foolish."

"And what's wrong with being a fool? Am I a fool for being a Catholic? Am I a fool for believing in the Church, for believing that's where I have to get married?"

"If you're such a believer, why do you have so little trouble exempting yourself from its teaching about sex? Sex outside of marriage?"

"I don't exempt myself. Can't you see that? That's what I'm talking about. I want to get married. Haven't you heard me? I want to get married. But I'm told I can't. So what do I do? Oh, yes, I know. I abstain. Abstinence. Continence. Why, when I'm more than willing, when I'm desperate to get married?" He squatted down again, his face inches from the priest. "Marry us. Then let me take care of her. She's going to die, but marry us first," he whispered.

Father Dunphy made no move. Slowly, Johnny stood up. His voice still close to a whisper, he said, "All right, then. I'm going to say something and I have to ask you not to look at me while I'm saying it. It could be proof that I'm the most trusting guy on the block or, worse, it could mean I've signed myself on to the biggest con job ever perpetrated in human history." He paused only slightly. Father Dunphy stared down at the bottom of the boat. "The real reason I want to marry Dempsey—why I want you to do the marrying—is that I was brought up to believe—and this is the hard part—is that I believe that marriage is a sacrament. It means we get special grace, special help when things get so difficult that we don't know what to do. For reasons I don't quite understand, I believe this. And I want that help—whatever form it might take—when the going gets really rough. The way it's going to."

Again he squatted down, again his face close to Father Dunphy's. "Whether my faith humbles me or humiliates me, I don't know. But I do know I want us—Dempsey and me—to have this help. If it really exists."

Father Dunphy, after a long look at Johnny, swung his body away, there on the seat of the rowing machine. He looked again at the footboard, then rested his feet against it.

Johnny bowed his head. "Please say something, Father."

The priest waited, then said, "May I sit here for a few minutes before I go?"

Without raising his head, Johnny said, "Would you be more comfortable up there, on the couch?"

"I'm fine here," he said quietly. "If it's all right. Just for a minute if you don't mind."

"I don't mind." Johnny stood up. "I'll get you something cold."

"No. Nothing. Please. Go finish your windows. I can find my own way out. Please. I'll be better here by myself."

After he'd taken a few steps back toward the windows, Johnny stopped. He thought he should say something, but he didn't know what it was. Maybe he should get the priest something to drink whether he said he wanted it or not. But he didn't want to interfere if the man preferred to be alone. He continued toward the windows, past the cupboards lining the walls where each man kept his civilian clothes, his personal belongings. Their doors needed painting. The pale green paint was worn or chipped away. His own cupboard, the third from the end, was no better than the rest. Near the padlock the wood showed, a honey-colored pine. One of the doors sagged slightly from a loose hinge. Noonan's door was worse; the screws securing the padlock were slipping out of their grooves and one hinge was pulled away from the frame completely.

The priest should not have seen this disrepair. He should not have been allowed to come up to this private space. He should not have seen the shredded wood of the floor or the collapsing couch. He should not have seen the television set with the smudged screen and the single sock on top.

When Johnny passed his cupboard, he straightened the lock so it wouldn't hang at an angle and stick out away from the hasp.

Quietly he tore some paper towels from the roll. He didn't want to disturb Father Dunphy. Quietly he crumpled them and began to rub away the dried glass wax he'd applied earlier. When the towel squeaked against the glass, he stopped, then put less pressure into his rubbing. He listened to hear the priest get up to leave, but heard nothing. Johnny's hope was that he'd turn around and Father Dunphy would be gone.

The inside windows were finished. While Johnny was raising the window so he could sit on the sill and do more outside, he decided he would stop trying to be so quiet. (Dempsey had—again and again—told him how noisy it was, trying to be quiet.) Ordinary sounds might help the priest make the necessary transfer back to ordinary life, away from the world of AIDS. It might help Johnny too.

He sat on the sill, outside. The priest was still sitting silently on the rowing machine, his back to Johnny, his feet still propped against the board in front of him. The window was lowered so the bottom of the frame rested on Johnny's thighs. He began his rubbing, clearing away the dusty dried wax. He kept his eyes focused a few inches from his nose. If the priest got up, Johnny would see it only as some movement in the distance, removed from the set range of his vision.

Now he could see through the clear glass into the room. Father Dunphy, slowly bending, slowly straightening himself, was rowing. Forward he bowed his head, then raised it, the seat moving back and forth as he pulled on the oars, released them, then pulled again. The massive shoulders, the broad back, leaned down, then brought themselves up, but so slowly, so evenly, that it seemed an act of keening, of mourning, of prayer.

Johnny went back to his work, but quiet again. When he finished, he sat there, looking through the separating glass. Father Dunphy had stopped rowing. He had let go of the oars and had put his open hands, palms down, on the seat. He didn't move.

Johnny raised the window and stepped inside. He waited to see if the priest might move. When nothing stirred, he turned back to the window and looked again to see where a smudge might be. He shifted to the side and looked from there. It was along the frame on the far side.

As he reached out his hand, he heard the priest say, "I'll marry you then, if that's what you want. And we'll let God, not the cardinal, decide whether it's valid or not." The man's back was still to Johnny. There had been a slight motion of the head, a lifting, as he'd said the words, but now no movement could be seen.

Johnny took a step forward, but before he could take a second step, the bell sounded, its pitch high and clear, the tiny hammer hitting against the metal disk. The priest made no move. Johnny quickly made a turn to his right, grabbed the pole and began the slide. His last sight of Father Dunphy was of a huge man becalmed in his boat, wondering how far he'd come and how far it was to an unseen shore.

4.

Johnny sat with Dempsey in Doctor Norstar's office. He was wearing his T-shirt with the Maltese Cross that identified him as a fireman. Experience had taught him that wearing some official marking at the doctor's office, at the clinic, at the hospital, got them, if not preferential treatment, at least an assurance that they wouldn't be made to wait beyond their turn. One might be tempted to keep the sick and the dying waiting, but not a fireman. Johnny would come with Dempsey whenever he could to make sure she got there with as little trouble as possible, to help her home if she was feeling wobbly, and to sit in on her sessions with Doctor Norstar so he'd be kept current with her condition and her treatment. He was also there for moral as well as physical support, especially if the news was to be less than encouraging, like the time Dempsey's T-cells fell to ninety-three from two hundred seventeen—meaning she was even more susceptible to infection than before. At moments like that, Johnny could casually rub his hand along her lower thigh or, once in a while, scratch her knee just to let her know he had heard and understood what Doctor Norstar had said. Dempsey herself took no notice of his ministrations and Johnny took this as a sign that they were acceptable and welcome.

Never when Doctor Norstar was talking did Dempsey

look at Johnny or in any way acknowledge his presence. Her face passive and her lips loosely touching each other, she would look at Doctor Norstar with an almost insulting indifference. It was left to Johnny to nod his head knowingly, to lift his chin to show that the information was being received into his consciousness. At times he could sense, but not prove, that his ears, already large and pulled somewhat away from his head, were bending ever so slightly forward, the better to hear the doctor's instruction.

And so it was that during their consultations, Johnny would be the one reaching, scratching, squeezing, nodding, straining, while Dempsey herself would limit her actions to an occasional blink, a slight flaring of the nostrils and, rarely, the raising of her right eyebrow. (The eyebrow was reserved for good news, the nostrils for bad, the blinks for the doctor's admonitions and instructions.)

Only after Doctor Norstar's dismissal, when they were in the elevator, would Dempsey take Johnny's arm in hers and shed the entire experience with a sigh that involved shoulders, chest, stomach, mouth, and ribs. She would then say something like, "Doctor Norstar looked tired the way she kept closing her eyes" or "Is Doctor Norstar losing weight?" or "Is Doctor Norstar gaining weight?" or "Do you think Doctor Norstar's coloring is just a little too pale?"—genuinely concerned, as if she had come there to check on the doctor's condition, to diagnose the doctor's difficulties and, once in a while, prescribe remedies: "She shouldn't drink so much coffee." "She could use a bacon cheeseburger and a side of fries." "She should lay off the pasta for a while." "A week in the Bahamas wouldn't hurt." No reference was made to what Doctor Norstar had said, no review of her prognostications, no comments on her commands, no speculations, no dismissals, no contradictions. Dempsey Coates had come to check up on the doctor, to offer her findings, express her concern and, with little hope that she would be obeyed, prescribe the necessary treatments.

Johnny would then draw her closer to his side as if it were a privilege beyond anyone's deserving, stare straight ahead and wish with all his might that they could lie down on the elevator floor and make slow love for the rest of their lives.

Today it was different. Johnny had determined that this was the day he'd ask Dempsey to marry him. He'd waited an entire day, afraid she'd not only say no but dismiss him from her service for having become so needy himself. But now he had his arguments ready—the leave of absence and, finally, Father Dunphy's offer.

He and Dempsey, as usual, sat on the orange leather couch in the waiting room. (Dempsey said it wasn't orange, it was yellow ochre. And it wasn't leather, it was Naugahyde.) He was reading and marking the lieutenant's manual for the test he hoped to take in the fall; she (of all things) was knitting. When Dempsey's diagnosis had predicted long hours in waiting rooms, she had searched out her knitting needles and some green yarn in which she'd hidden her mother's wedding ring. (Her mother had hocked whatever jewelry she had, including the engagement ring that Dempsey only dimly remembered from seeing it in the soap dish in the bathroom until, one day, it too disappeared.)

There had been enough green yarn for a single mitten. Unable to match the color, Dempsey had knitted a corresponding red mitten and would wear them, whatever the weather, from Christmas until Three Kings. During this time she would also wear the wedding ring—third finger, left hand, where it belonged—and would then retire it and the mittens, the ring shoved into the thumb of the green mitten, held in place by a moth ball, until the end of the following Advent, when they would again be called into service, warming her hands, decorating her finger.

Dempsey was, at the moment, knitting herself a bulky turtleneck, a darker green than the mitten. Assuming that sooner or later weight loss would bring creases to her neck, and since her neck was the one vanity she allowed herself beside her buttocks, the sweater would conceal the creases and permit her to indulge in the narcissism, the self-appreciation that had been one of life's little satisfactions since she was six.

So insistently did the needle points flash in and out of Johnny's peripheral vision that he shifted away from Dempsey, pretending that he could deal with the lieutenant's manual only if the book was resting on his right knee. It was then that he saw the child crawl out from behind the receptionist's desk—a counter, really—that separated computers, cabinets, phones, faxes, and the receptionist herself from the waiting patients, a protective barrier fending off the powerless from the powerful.

The child, a boy somewhere between two and three, seemed a little too old to be creeping and crawling, but perhaps he had been exploring off-limits territory and was still trying to avoid detection. Caught in his right hand was a small stuffed tiger—a trophy of the hunt—which he pressed down onto the linoleum floor with each forward move, emphasizing the brutality of the capture. He was wearing overalls—yellow corduroy—the bib and straps holding in place a pale blue flannel shirt decorated with small clowns that made the shirt look suspiciously like a pajama top. His light brown hair was mostly uncombed, with a cowlick sticking up in back like a small tepee.

He raised his head and used the tiger to wipe hair from his eyes. Instead of looking directly at Johnny or at Dempsey, he gazed just to the side of them, too polite to stare, too proud to declare his interest. He veered to his right and crawled away from them, keeping close to the counter. After the tiger had been squashed down onto the floor two more times, the boy stopped and stood up. He looked taller standing, perhaps because the legs of his overalls were too short, showing bright blue socks sticking out of his well-worn sneakers, one of which was untied. For a few moments, he plucked at the tiger's fur, trying to restore its nap after the squeezing and squashing it had just endured at his hand. After he stopped, he kept his fingers resting on the animal's back, then looked up, staring directly at Dempsey.

Dempsey, as far as Johnny could tell, hadn't seen the child at all. She was clattering away with her needles as if some evil overseer might come at any moment and accuse her of malingering. Johnny considered saying something to the boy, but felt it would make him an unwanted intruder coming between the child and Dempsey. With his yellow marker he purposely noted a passage in the manual that was of no importance whatsoever, then increased his concentration on what he was supposed to be studying.

When the boy rushed past him, to his left, Johnny was aware only of the overalls and the sleeves of the pale blue shirt. He felt the weight of the flung body against his side and saw the untied sneaker as it slid over the page of his manual, forcing it to the floor. The boy's knee dug into his leg as his elbow knocked against his ear. The sounds he heard were half whimper, half grunt, then Dempsey's voice saying, "Wha . . . ?"

The boy was hitting the stuffed tiger against Dempsey's cheek. One of the knitting needles kept jabbing Johnny in the arm, then poked him in the side, its rhythms set by the repeated motions of the boy's flailing. "Please! Don't —" Dempsey had pulled her head back, but the boy, after two blows against Dempsey's neck, found again the side of her face and was banging the tiger against her cheek, her nose, her eye, the sounds rising in pitch, more whimper now than grunt.

Johnny jumped up and grabbed the boy just above the waist. Before he could pull him away completely, he had punched Dempsey's shoulder, her breast, and the half-knitted sweater, leaving the tiger itself tangled in the yarn as if it had escaped into the protections of the high grass. Dempsey got one last kick against her leg just as Johnny swung the boy away, lifting him higher so that his feet, now peddling the air, could do less damage.

By now Daphne the receptionist, Anne the nurse, and Doctor Norstar herself had crowded around and were repeating over and over again what was apparently the child's name, Joey. A stout woman who had been reading a magazine let the magazine rest on her lap and was taking in the scene with complete indifference. Johnny held the boy out away from him as if afraid he might pee on him. A gaunt young man with short-cropped hair crossed his arms over his lap and was resting his head. He brought one shoulder up, trying to cover an ear and shut out the noise. Dempsey herself was trying to extricate the tiger from the tangled yarn without letting any stitches slip from the needles.

"Here. I'll take him." Doctor Norstar reached out to Joey and placed her hands just below Johnny's, firmly taking hold at the waist. As the doctor drew the child to herself, the boy began to cry. "What are you crying about?" the doctor asked. "*You* weren't hurt. And why were you doing—doing that to Miss Coates?"

Doctor Norstar lowered Joey to the floor and the wail diminished to a whimper. "Daphne," the doctor said, her voice finding, even in the confusion, the tone of concerned authority that Johnny considered one of her greater gifts, "Take him into my office. I'll be right there." She then turned to the child. "Run along with Daphne, unless you want to apologize first to Miss Coates for being so naughty."

Joey turned toward Dempsey. He watched the tiger being freed from the yarn. "Coats?" the boy said. "Like raincoats?" He moved closer to Dempsey so he could observe the phenomenon at closer range.

Dempsey could only stare. Daphne took the child's hand and was easing him toward the hall that led to Doctor Norstar's office. Dempsey tried to smooth the sweater out over her lap, then examined the needles for dropped stitches.

"She resents you because you're the one getting all her mother's attention," Johnny said.

Dempsey stared down at her knitting. Her face was still. "I know. But I was so scared. I thought it was my little boy—grown to that age, come to get even with me for giving him AIDS. But it wasn't him." She paused, then added softly, "If only it had been."

Before Johnny could say anything, she resumed knitting, a plea that Johnny say nothing—at least for now. But he had to do something—offer some comfort—make some gesture of understanding, state his own exasperated plea that he be allowed to take up some share of her hauntings. Before he could sort out his options and arrive at any particular insistence, Doctor Norstar came over and sat down on the chair just on the other side of the end table.

Slowly she lowered herself, with utmost control, as if worried that she might collapse into the seat. "I'll take the blame for that one," she said. "I had to bring him with me. A pipe burst at Day Care, I couldn't get hold of Inez, and her father's got a case in court. Sorry." She was speaking through the philodendron on the table, making some of the leaves stir. Johnny's plea would have to wait. Dempsey turned toward Doctor Norstar. A leaf touched her nose. She shifted her body closer to Johnny. "It's all right," Dempsey said quickly. "I'm fine." She took a deep breath and let it out, raising and lowering her entire torso to reinforce the effort. She looked down at the sweater bunched on her lap. "I understand," she whispered.

"Thanks." Doctor Norstar held out a hand toward the knitting needles. "But if you could hold off for just a minute. The needles going like that make me talk too fast." She shoved the plant back farther on the table so she could have a better view of her patient.

Dempsey turned to look at the doctor, no longer shielded by the leaves. She lowered the needles onto her lap. To Johnny the doctor's smile seemed now not an indulgent benevolence bestowed on an intractable patient, but a determined effort to conceal a weariness, an attempt to contradict an obvious truth: Doctor Norstar, uninfected, free of any virus that might inflict itself on her sturdy young body, was nonetheless being consumed by the pestilence that surrounded her. Untouched by actual contagion, she was still not immune to the depletions, the wasting, and the brave hypocrisies that plagued her patients. She, too, it seemed to Johnny, had experienced the denials and anger and had come at last to this sad acceptance that—if one was lucky—marked the final phase of the illness. She, too, was being consumed; she, too, had experienced the rack, the rage, the drained energy seeping away, the need to lie down with only one final plea—that she be excused from having to rise again, ever.

Slowly Dempsey's hand rose from her lap. She was reaching toward Doctor Norstar's face but stopped just after it had begun the curve that would bring the hand to the doctor's cheek. Johnny could see Dempsey in profile, still turned toward the doctor. Maybe it was because some color had come into her cheeks, or her terror, still there, had drawn the flesh smoothly back to show the fine high cheekbone, the slightly swollen lips, the curved line that flowed from her chin, along her neck, to her throat. Her ear, glimpsed through her hair, seemed heartbreaking because it was so unaware of itself. Dempsey, as always, was transcendently beautiful.

Now, even with the doctor there, was surely the time to ask her to marry him. He couldn't help it. He had to ask her now, in this moment of her unbearable perfection. But again he waited one moment too long. "Can't we go now?" Dempsey said.

"Yes, of course." Doctor Norstar pulled the philodendron back into position. The session was over. She smoothed her starched white smock and shifted her feet out from under her chair. She was getting ready to stand up. Dempsey was shoving her unfinished sweater, yarn, and needles down into the sailcloth bag. The words "Guggenheim Museum Downtown" were stenciled on its side. It was the tote she lugged with her just about everywhere—including the bathroom—when she was worried that she might be kept waiting. She stood up.

"No. Wait," Doctor Norstar said. She was laughing.

"What are we doing? You have an appointment. I haven't seen you yet."

Johnny and Dempsey, too, and for a moment, Doctor Norstar, had forgotten. The doctor headed down the hall to her office. Johnny and Dempsey followed. Daphne, Joey in tow, came out. Joey backed against the wall, his arms flat against it. "Go on, Joey, go on," Daphne said, but Joey didn't move. When Dempsey and Johnny passed him, Johnny heard Joey say, "Her name is Coats. Like raincoats."

The elevator moved down slowly. Perhaps this was in deference to those who should be spared anything that might rattle or jar. Or it could be that the prolonged ride was provided as a special courtesy, a mercy for those who needed a suspended state where adjustment, assimilations, could be made, where preparations could be formulated and decisions made. In this intervening time, fate could be embraced or refused, or simply stared in the face. Reprieves could be given, stunned acknowledgments made, the foot made firm, the eyes hardened, and the heart prepared.

The elevator stopped at the fourth floor and two chatty and cheerful women got on. Dempsey let out an aggrieved sigh and pulled her tote bag closer to her stomach. Doctor Norstar had told them to return—yet again—to the third floor of St. Vincent's clinic for yet another round of blood work. The lab had—yet again—confused the tests. The results sent over in Dempsey's name were obviously not hers.

"But why can't they be my tests?" Dempsey had asked.

"Not possible." The doctor had shaken her head.

"But my T-cells have gone up and down, up and

down from the beginning."

"Not like this. Take my word for it. I don't know what this person was having blood work for, but it wasn't for any virus or any infection. I'll tell you that. Everything is completely normal. I want you to have more good days than bad days, but this. . . . Well, it just plain shouldn't have your name on it. You have to go back. Sorry. Truly."

"But they made this mistake the last time I—"

"I know. The switch is obviously persisting. I talked to Flocene and she's going to follow through herself, step by step, so the correction can he made. Think of the other guy—the one who might be given *your* results."

"True. But I'm the one who has to sit for—"

"Not this time. Go straight to the third floor. Flocene's expecting you. You're next. I still have some pull."

"But how can they keep making the same—"

"Guess. Just guess." Doctor Norstar moved her head a little closer to Dempsey and simply kept looking at her, not moving. There was, under each eye, a downward crease, formed, it would seem, by the color draining from the eye itself. The eyes were able to hold their stare now only because they seemed too tired to close.

Dempsey pulled back in her chair and shook her head. When she spoke, her voice was quiet, "It's dangerous getting everything all mixed up like this."

"Tell me." Doctor Norstar stood up. "You going with her?" she asked Johnny.

"No. He's not going with me," Dempsey said. "I should certainly know the way by this time."

"I'm going with her," Johnny said. "Just for the fun of it."

When the elevator doors opened onto the lobby, Dempsey cut past the two women and went quickly toward the entrance. Johnny, equally unmindful of etiquette, stepped off in front of the women and caught up with Dempsey. She was already at the heavy glass door and was reaching out for the handle. Johnny's hand started toward the door, but he stopped. Patiently he stood there and waited until Dempsey had opened the door. She went through first and held it open for him. He considered saying thank you but said instead, "Will you marry me?" Dempsey neither slowed nor quickened her pace as she headed down the street toward the corner, nor did she look at Johnny.

She let her knee knock rhythmically against the tote bag, each step sending it out ahead of her as if to clear the way for her approach. This meant she was thinking.

5.

"I want to go with you. I really do. I like Winnie." Johnny and Dempsey had come out of the clinic onto Seventh Avenue. Dempsey was pressing the wide Band-Aid stuck across the crook of her arm, checking for any blood that might seep through. None came. She moved her bag to her other hand and pulled down the sleeve of her shirt. The bag kept bumping against her side. Johnny reached over and helped with the sleeve, fussing a little at the wrist to make the task seem more difficult than it was.

"Maybe you like Winnie," Dempsey said, "but you hate her paintings."

"I don't hate her paintings."

"You scorn them."

"I don't scorn them."

"You dismiss them."

"Maybe we should go home."

"Why home when you're panting to see Winnie's paintings?"

"They took a lot of your blood."

"Of course they took a lot of my blood." She laughed. "Didn't you know? Bloodletting is back. They've realized that what most people need is a good healthy loss of blood. But they can't come right out and say it. Sounds too medieval. So what they do is say they've got to take all these tests. So you go and they take blood. Then they take more blood. But they're not testing for anything. They're bloodletting, good old-fashioned bloodletting. Maybe this is a trial for the cure but they can't admit it's an experiment. So they invent test after test after test. Take the blood. Take more blood. Then more. Don't stop. They're not testing for anything. It's a cover, that's all. I wasn't tested just now. That was a bloodletting session, nothing more. And nothing less. And see what it did for me? When have I felt better? When have I looked better? Bloodletting. It's back. Maybe this time it's here to stay."

"I still think we should go home."

"No. Winnie's waiting. And I actually feel like I'm in stunning good health. But you have to promise me. No leeches. No matter what. In the end, they'll probably want to apply leeches. Promise you won't let them."

Johnny persisted, "If you don't show up, Winnie will understand."

"You don't know Winnie. And besides, the walk will do you good. You've been sitting like a slug most of the day."

"We'll start and then see how far you feel like going. Okay?"

"Fine with me. If I fall in a heap, we take a taxi. There's money in my purse if I'm not responding to external stimuli."

When they got to the corner, Johnny put the knitting bag under his left arm. Never could he bring himself to carry a shopping bag or any other receptacle by the handles, the tote bag included. To him, a bag with handles was too much like a purse. The tote was an enlarged purse. And he could not walk down the street carrying a purse. Held against him, the tote was just a bag, like a grocery bag. He could carry a grocery bag. If he held a tote bag this way, he was allowed to carry it. But only if he held it this way.

They stepped down from the curb, then back up again as an ambulance came tweeting and hawking along Twelfth Street. It hesitated at Seventh, at the red light, then swung in a wide arc to the Emergency entrance on the far side of the avenue, almost down to Eleventh. Now the traffic light changed and they'd have to wait.

Johnny was tempted to ask Dempsey if she'd heard him when he'd asked her to marry him, but he knew he'd better not. Of course she'd heard. One thing he'd learned was never to repeat a question. There was no need. Dempsey would answer when she knew the answer. If she didn't say anything, it was because she was in the process of finding out what it was she wanted to say. Sometimes this would take a few minutes, other times it might take a few days. But sooner or later she would answer. Seldom did she ask for clarifications. It was Johnny's impression that she would prefer to do the clarifying herself, asking and answering subsidiary questions in the privacy of her own mind, like a mathematician working her way step by step through an equation, keeping silent until the deed was done and the problem solved.

At some moment, today, tomorrow, the next day, Dempsey would give him a simple yes, a simple no, probably without preface, certainly without explanation. Meantime, he would leave her to herself, knowing she was, even as they stood there, hard at work.

The light changed. They crossed the street, barely escaping a Jeep Wrangler making a right turn. When they got to the other side, Johnny cupped his hand under Dempsey's elbow.

"Careful. You're grabbing," she said.

"I like to grab."

"In that case, okay."

She reached over and pulled his hand under her elbow and placed it along her arm. She pressed her own arm closer to her side, a quick squeeze to signal acceptance. Johnny felt, for the moment the squeeze lasted, the soft give of her breast, then the release—charged with the possibility that it could happen again. He surrendered to euphoria. He was walking down the street, arm in arm with Dempsey Coates. More than this he asked neither of heaven nor of earth. This, even more than their lovemaking, made him feel that history had fulfilled itself in their union. Toward this moment all happenings had tended; the past had no purpose but to provide and prepare for this. It was only Dempsey's hold that kept him bound to earth, that prevented his immediate assumption into the skies.

The gallery was crowded. It was on the ground floor but Johnny didn't doubt that Dempsey would have had trouble with a few flights of stairs. She had spent the entire walk gawking, checking the sky as if for messages, staring into shop windows, interested in whatever wares were on display: shoes, toys, lamps, books, magazines. It seemed that she wanted to make sure the items were there in their places, where they belonged and could be found whenever she might have need of them. Then she'd move on. At the Vesuvio Bakery on Prince Street, her head jerking like a bird's from one kind of bread to another, she made Johnny go inside and buy a round loaf while she continued to take inventory outside. He held it out to her, unwrapped. Without saying anything, she sniffed it, then stuck it in the tote bag, not caring that some of the flour was brushed off onto the knitting.

The only difficult moment came when they passed a deserted warehouse. Dempsey had stopped and looked at a metal door leading to an outside passageway. Razor wire was rolled over the top of the door. When Johnny had asked why she was stopping, she explained that, for a moment, she had thought that this was the Lunch Room. Then she remembered that the Lunch Room was farther downtown, almost in her own neighborhood.

She had explained to Johnny that the Lunch Room was where she had gone to get her drugs. One day Dempsey had pointed it out to him during one of their walks: the iron door, the rolled razor wire. She told him about the spiffy clientele, about her own participation in its revels. When they had turned the corner, a man in a linen suit, light blue shirt, slant-striped tie, and soft leather shoes was coming toward them. When he came closer, there was the slightest break in the rhythm of Dempsey's step. Johnny knew where the man was going. And he knew that the man and Dempsey had "done" lunch together.

The guests in the gallery for Winnie's opening were dressed in varying hues of drab. Outright black, the preferred statement of recent times, was only intermittently represented. If any color threatened to be vibrant or assertive, it had been pitilessly bleached or faded. Blues had become grays, reds were tan, greens another shade of gray, and yellows drained to what could only be called dirty. Maybe there had been a fear that the clothing might distract from the hair. The man with green hair, the woman with purple, didn't count. Fashion had left them behind. Most of the women had had their hair twisted and tormented into long and skinny corkscrew strands inspired, it seemed, by the snakes of the Medusa or the tails of some very scrawny pigs. And now some of the men, the younger ones, had taken up the cause. Uncombed was hardly a new idea, but this was not uncombed. This hair had obviously been treated with some substance that would not let it rest. It must tangle with itself, it must spring out and away from the ear as if fearing contagion, it must, on the top, be a nest built by a drunken wren, and most of all, the hair must be black. It must be blacker than black, stopping just this side of purple. The old black garments had found, perhaps, their lost expression splayed out from the scalp, its source the brain itself, that lobe which nourishes vanity in all its guises.

The talk was small bites of chatter, like the sound of someone munching crackers. "Mingle," Dempsey said. "You in front, me in back. And get some wine if you want. None for me. And tell the bartender to hide the tote. I don't want anyone to know I knit. Of course, they might think it's you. That I wouldn't mind. But do what you want. There's Winnie." Dempsey twisted her way through the crowd, turning in one direction, then another, her hips leading the way.

There, indeed, was Winnie—tall and of a certain amplitude, with long lightly waved hair streaming down past her shoulders. She was wearing a gauzy tan dress with floppy sleeves and a shawl or a veil or whatever it might be thrown over her left shoulder and caught in the crook of her right arm. It was Winnie's way to drape herself, and only the day's heat must have persuaded her to limit her swathing. Even so, the light material of her dress and her shawl floated and flowed around her considerable bulk like admiring attendants, touching her, withdrawing, returning to whisper again and again reassurances of her beauty, of her delicacy, of the sweetness of her enviable flesh.

Dempsey had made her way through the throng. She and Winnie were kissing each other on both cheeks, once with the nose and once with the mouth. Johnny decided it was time to look at the paintings.

To his surprise, they were astonishing, and beautiful. Winnie knew how to see. And more than see. Each painting seemed the creation and fulfillment of its own universe, a core of color expanding outward, widening into new and ever more vibrant color. Each painting a searching, a yearning ever outward into infinity. In the beginning was not only light; there was color. And he would never have known that if Winnie hadn't told him. Why had he not appreciated her work before? Was it because, after having been granted permission to marry Dempsey in a Catholic ceremony, he was now in some kind of altered state of consciousness?

The woman Johnny found to mingle with was named Bianca. She had smooth dark skin in which Johnny could actually detect a tinge of green. He'd often heard of olive-colored skin, but to make the concept applicable he'd had to assume—until now—that the olives were black or dark brown. Now he realized they might actually be green. Bianca, no doubt about it, had olive- colored skin and it seemed entirely right: only the Mediterranean sky, the Mediterranean soil could have produced the flesh that softly rounded her cheeks; only the Mediterranean sun could have trained those eyelids to raise themselves no more than half way.

"Those beautiful animals in the morning light," Bianca was saying, "the backstretch, you can hardly see it in the morning mist, the horses not racing, just running, cantering, exercising, appearing out of the mist, disappearing into it, and you sit there near the rail and have your coffee. Magical."

She was describing breakfast at the Saratoga track, which was right next door to an artists' retreat she'd gone to the previous August. This, he knew, was her way of assuring him that she was sensitive, susceptible to nature's glories.

"Only one thing you have to watch out for," she continued. "You have to be careful who you go with. It's so beautiful, so stirring, that whoever you go with, you're going to fall in love." Her smile tightened. "I know," she whispered. "One morning I went all by myself and it worked. I could hardly keep my hands off for a week."

Johnny opened his mouth to indicate a laugh, kept it open long enough to give an accurate measure of his appreciation, then closed it. "Maybe I'd better not go," he said. "At least not by myself. I used to have problems in that area."

"That's understandable," Bianca said.

Johnny, through experience, was becoming more and more adept at transitions, at guiding a conversation from a closing sentence to an opening one. He was about to ask her about the artists' retreat. That could keep her going until Dempsey would be ready to leave. "Tell me," he said—then saw out of the corner of his eye a young man looking at one of the paintings. He was smiling, not just with his lips, but with his whole face. His cheeks, his forehead, all flesh, all muscles, seemed lifted up. His eyes were possessing the painting. They were taking it in, consuming it. Johnny expected him to start gagging if he didn't stop. He wanted to move closer so he'd be there, at the man's side, when the gagging began so he could help him catch his breath again. He made the slightest move in the young man's direction.

Bianca, without the need of inquiry, had begun to tell him about the retreat, the solitude, the lakes, the lunches. As she was expanding on the subject of fresh carrot sticks, the young man whirled toward them as if Bianca and Johnny had called his name. His eyes still holding the vision of what he'd seen, he said, "They're Coptic? Can you see? They're Coptic!" Without waiting for either Johnny or Bianca to ask what, in this instance, Coptic meant, he continued, "Decorative. All decorative. Nothing but decorative in the morning, decorative in the evening, decorative in the summertime. But the Copts—for them the decorative wasn't to embellish but to conceal. It had a purpose beyond pleasure. You know that. I know that. I don't have to tell you. They weren't allowed to display the Cross. They had to hide it, to paint, to sculpt elaborations, filigrees, distractions, exquisite patterns, unending labyrinths to prove that the Cross wasn't really there. But it was, it was. And all the elaborations, they became a homage, they were praise as laughter, a cunning adoration. Mockery as veneration. And there, there in the painting, do you see it? The Cross. Not visible, hidden, but it's there. Look. See it? Where's the artist? Which one? Lead me so I can fall down and worship."

His eyes were fevered, his lips dry and beginning to crack. And as he'd been speaking, Johnny saw the brown lesions—some with a tinge of pink, on his face, on his neck, on his forehead, and on the backs of his hands. He saw the skin drawn taut over the skull, the caved-in cheeks, the bones pushing outward beneath the eyes. If the young man failed to relax, if he persisted in his vision, surely the skin would split and curl away, exposing the naked bones beneath.

"Is the artist here?" His eyes were pleading now, frightened that his wish would be denied. Before Johnny could point to Winnie at the far end of the room, the man stumbled close to Johnny. "Where?" he asked, his voice a rasping whisper. Tears had welled up into his eyes. He took hold of Johnny's shoulders.

The next breaths were a quick succession of drawn-in wheezes with no exhalations. Still struggling to speak, the man took in yet more air, the wheeze weaker than before. Johnny reached out his hand, not sure where to apply it. To ward Johnny off, the coughs began, not deep and rumbling, but weak, confined to the throat and the neck. They sounded fake, the kind of cough used to comment, to punctuate. Were the man not gasping for air, the coughs would seem no more than a nervous clearing of the throat. And yet he was still smiling and it seemed the choking had been induced by uncontrollable laughter.

Johnny reached his hand behind the young man, but hesitated to touch his back. Then he touched it, tapping lightly just to let him know the hand was there. In acknowledgment, the man nodded even as the coughing continued. Johnny tapped again, not harder, but with his whole hand, now a pat on the back. Again the man nodded, still sucking in air through the constricted passages that wheezed their fury at the intrusion, still the gleeful cough struggling to become an outright laugh.

Bianca had drawn away to give the man room. The pats on the back continued with growing force, bringing the man closer to Johnny by slow degrees. The pats became firmer, more insistent, a warning to the cough to abandon this man. Still harder Johnny hit, drawing the man closer. Johnny could feel dry spurts of breath aimed at his face. The man's fevered eyes glared into Johnny's eyes. Gently Johnny brought the man to himself, guiding the head to his left so it could rest on his shoulder. Two wisps of hair were curled behind the man's ear, another wisp, higher on the dome of the skull, rose straight up, then fell, resting on the crown of the balding head. Near the ear were two lesions, pinker than those on the man's face, like large paramecia stranded in a frozen waste.

With the tip of his nose Johnny touched first one lesion then the other. Into the man's ear he whispered, "Shhhh. Shhhh." Then, relaxing his lips, he pressed them against one of the lesions, against the dry flesh. "Shhhh. Shhhh." Slowly he rocked the man back and forth. The wheezing, the coughing, the laughter had stopped.

The man, like someone awakening from a light sleep, pulled away from Johnny's hold. "You're Johnny the fireman," he said. "You're with Dempsey." He reached out and touched Johnny's cheek. "You poor man," he said. "You poor, poor man."

Before Johnny could say anything back, he felt a soft prod in his side. Dempsey had shoved the tote bag at him. "It's time to take up my knitting again." Johnny took the bag. He was still looking at the man. The man's eyes were blank, emptied of what they'd seen. The vision, the Coptic Crosses, were no longer there. He was at peace.

Dempsey put her arm in Johnny's and steered him toward the door. Johnny hesitated. The man had exhorted him to look at the paintings, at the Coptic labyrinths Winnie had so cunningly devised. Johnny wanted to look now; he wanted to assure himself that the man hadn't been raving, that he had seen what was there and had brought himself near to death to proclaim its truth. But Dempsey seemed eager to leave.

Outside, walking west on Spring Street, Johnny could smell the bread in the top of the knitting bag. As they were crossing Wooster Street, Dempsey pulled her arm away and scratched her nose, then returned the arm. "You were beautiful just now, with that man," she said quietly.

"He couldn't stop coughing."

"Sure. But you were the one who cared. I didn't see anyone else ready to get himself coughed all over."

"No big deal."

Dempsey stopped there on the sidewalk, thought a minute, then started walking again. "It's something to see, what the epidemic's done. How some people respond. If you didn't know he had AIDS, would you have helped him like that?"

"I don't know."

"We read about it all the time. People brought closer together." She paused, then added, "Like us. If it weren't for the epidemic . . . Well, you know the rest."

"Then I'm supposed to be grateful for the epidemic?"

"Well, aren't you?"

Now it was Johnny who stopped. He paused, took one more step, stopped again and, without looking at Dempsey, said, "If it took this epidemic to get us together again, I have to hope I'd never have seen you again, that we'd never have gotten together again. Ever."

"I'm not sure that's what you're supposed to say."

"Then I'll say it again. If I can only walk down this street with you because of AIDS, then I have to wish I wouldn't be walking down this street now, with you here and me with you. Nothing is worth this epidemic, nothing pays anyone for what you—and that guy too—what you're going through, you or anyone else who is sick."

He was still looking straight ahead, but Dempsey half turned her head so she could see him. He took in a deep breath through his nose, then exhaled, but slowly. "Give AIDS nothing. If it takes all this to make some of us act decent for a change, then let us *never* act decent. If it takes AIDS to change people for the better, let them stay pricks always. Nothing—I mean *no thing* compensates. We can do without whatever it is, without whatever good might come of it. Not if it takes the epidemic to make it happen."

"And that includes me? I mean, includes us?"

Johnny tightened his jaw, then reached over and put her arm through his. "We should get you home. It's getting late." Again they walked, Dempsey casually, thoughtfully, Johnny breathing a little heavily after his outburst. He was carrying the tote bag at his right side, holding it by the handles, now uncaring about its resemblance to a purse. Dempsey swayed her body, bumping her hip against his. She lowered her head, then raised it. "Watching you with him, I was reminded of something I keep forgetting."

"Oh?"

"I get so—well—so self-absorbed thinking about myself all the time. Just in case you hadn't noticed. We all—all of us—well, all of us dying like this—we forget to think about anything else. Anyone else. But watching you with him—the strangest thing—I remembered something I don't want to forget."

"What's that?"

Dempsey gave a short laugh that heaved her chest up, then quickly down. "How much I love you. Imagine. How could I ever forget a thing like that?" She shook her head, unable to believe such an unbelievable fact. "Oh—and by the way—yes, of course I'll marry you."

Johnny burst into tears.

"Well," Dempsey said, "nothing like making a man happy."

Johnny sniffed, then laughed, then sniffed again, laughed some more, and let the tears fall where they may.

6.

This was Dempsey's favorite part of a trip to Staten Island. The ferry was getting closer and closer to the slip but was headed full throttle toward the thick weathered planking that framed the manmade cove where the boat would dock. The motor stopped; the ferry kept its course at a barely lessened speed toward the pilings. Dempsey decided to stay exactly where she was, at the rail of the bow—if a ferry can be said to have a bow—and experience the usual crash.

She wished Johnny had joined her by now. He'd wanted to study and had found himself a bench—they looked more like pews—about a third of the way back, away from the front deck but still not too close to the concession stand. Other passengers were already streaming through the forward doors, not to disembark, it seemed, but to witness along with Dempsey the boat's slam into the planking. She turned to look for Johnny but saw only a late-morning crowd of overweight people, two women with strollers, one tall man wearing a baseball cap backwards even though he was close to fifty, two teenage boys, their legs spread, their feet braced firmly on the deck, eager to test their balance against the coming crash. Everyone except Dempsey seemed to be staring at the two metal claw-like suspensions reaching out over the water, ready to snatch the boat the minute it came within their grasp. They were, she knew, the mechanical gangplanks that would connect the docked ferry to the terminal, but they seemed more predator than welcoming arms at the moment.

The ferry rammed into the piling. Everyone on deck took two quick steps to the right, then one step to the left, between which each had made a half-step toward the cabin and a half-step toward the terminal. The planking creaked and squealed, leaning back at a twenty-degree angle, complaining rather than accusing, almost bored at this repeated indignity. In retaliation the planks shoved the boat into position for proper docking. By now, equilibrium had been re-established among the passengers and there was the general stir toward the gates. The boat's engines reversed, sending a heavy shudder through the entire vessel as if the ferry were loath to do what it must do now: touch the Staten Island shore.

The shuddering stopped, the ferry glided silently, obediently, into the rounded slip. The metal claws lowered, making their claim. A sandy-haired man wearing workman's gloves shoved half the accordion gate back against the rail, then shoved the other half in the opposite direction. The gateway to Staten Island was open. The passengers, neither eager nor reluctant, began the climb across the humped metal gangplanks, no one pushing, no one pausing.

Someone took Dempsey's hand. It was Johnny, the dog-eared manual gripped in his other hand, held against his thigh, the masculine way of carrying a book. They let themselves be caught up into the orderly throng that was skirting the sides of the terminal building, nosing themselves toward the bus stops with the unhurried collectivity of cows or sheep. (Johnny's car, a fifteen-year-old Volkswagen Rabbit he'd bought from his brother-in-law, had muffler problems. In Manhattan, this was no special difficulty, but Johnny, as a native of Staten Island, could hardly be expected to pollute the township's quiet with the explosive chugging of a motor unmuffled. The car was left behind. They would take the bus.)

"You learn anything?" Dempsey asked.

"A forty-point-three-cubic-foot Air Pac tested at three pounds of air pressure will weigh thirty pounds."

"How fascinating?" She yawned and then laughed.

Today Dempsey would meet Johnny's family. As the only child of a single mother whose full-time career was playing the horses, she had not all that often wondered what it would have been like to be a part of a family—a real family. She had been more curious than envious, but now she would finally find out.

She and Johnny had agreed not to mention the intended marriage, or Dempsey's illness. The family, in each instance, would be informed all in good time. And yet, relieved of even these specific concerns, Dempsey must expect some assault on her nerves. His family could despise her. She and Johnny were, after all, living together, unmarried—and Johnny was, to begin with, the baby brother; they could despise her. She could be questioned beyond her patience—her parentage, her past, her religion, her art, how she did her hair. Anything might happen. It might be a disaster for everyone.

And there was, as well, her illness and the not always suppressed concern about its unpredictability. Since her diagnosis, the least gurgle in her intestine, the slightest whistle in her breath, the first hint of bloat, anything at all could convince her that another skirmish had begun or, quite possibly, that the final onslaught was underway. A name forgotten, the sudden realization that there had been a moment for which her memory could not account, the reluctance of a word to surface in her brain—all this had come to announce the arrival of dementia. An unearned weariness, a yeasty thickening in her mouth, the sudden soiling of her underclothes, all were warnings—sometimes blared, sometimes whispered—that the next great battle might already be engaged, ready or not. And today could be the day.

At the moment, there was no gurgle, no whistle, no incipient bloat, and words seemed to be there when she needed them. As a matter of fact, lately she'd been having some better days. But she knew from experience these respites were too good to last. A fact was a fact. But something was always about to happen. And when it did, she must be prepared if not to avoid it, then to accept it with as much good grace as the occasion might allow. If anything related to her illness happened, Johnny's family could easily learn more about her than had been planned for this initial visit. That would be fine with her. *Anything,* she decided, would be fine with her. Ahead of them now, on a rise directly behind the terminal, was Borough Hall, a cement-columned red-brick building with sad pretensions to stateliness. Behind that the island rose at a steep pitch and, Dempsey had been told, Johnny's mother's house was almost at the top.

"You shouldn't have! Maury, come look. From Dempsey. You really shouldn't have. But, oh Patricia, come look. It's the most gorgeous ever. A treasure. An absolute treasure. Theresa, don't you want to see?"

Johnny's mother was holding against her wrist the antique bracelet Dempsey had brought her, a silver rose intricately woven into a braid of stems and leaves. (No thorns.) Dempsey wasn't sure about the "gorgeous" but she did know that it was a treasure—and had the receipt to prove it. She'd found it—after a lengthy search—in a shop on Canal Street where the owner, one remove from a pawnbroker, claimed to be a dealer in "antique jewelry." Johnny's mother was named Rose, and Dempsey had been unable to avoid the obvious.

And now the bracelet was doing its job in exactly the way Dempsey had hoped it would. Not for nothing had the tradition of gift-giving been instituted. Johnny's sisters—Maureen, Patricia, Theresa—were all crowded around their mother, with Johnny beaming over Maureen's shoulder. They, along with Johnny's mother, were oohing and aahing over the bracelet, passing it from hand to hand, turning it over, holding it up to the light, draping it over a wrist, balancing it on the tip of a finger. Dempsey had, with this simple generosity, deflected everyone's attention at the crucial moment of their meeting. No one was paying the least mind to her, only to the gift. She was not being subjected to the terrible scrutiny that would have been inflicted on her had she not given the bracelet—at least not inflicted yet. She would have time to make adjustments; she would be allowed to study the sisters, the mother, and Johnny himself, a switch in ritual that only gift-giving could achieve.

Quickly—because there was only so much time—Dempsey noted that the sisters were pretty but not beautiful. Maureen, the oldest, had auburn hair, but the nose was too regal for a face without more prominent cheekbones. Theresa was the one with the big brown eyes, but her face was triangular, diminishing to a tiny pointed chin. And she had too much hair, a profusion of light brown. To Dempsey she looked like a fox trying to be a lion. Patricia, the middle sister, came closest to being a beauty. For her the regal nose had been fitted between two fine cheekbones; for her the mouth had been lengthened and plumped up a bit. Like Johnny, she had deep blue eyes and, for her as for Johnny, the determined chin that was not allowed to stick out too far. But, also like Johnny, she had sand-colored hair. On him, it seemed pleasingly coarse—a sexy indifference to gloss and to shine. But for Patricia, it seemed a deprivation. Should she ever be tempted to consider herself beautiful or perfect, she had only to take note of her coarse hair and the temptation would be beaten back for good. In this way, Patricia's sandy hair was a form of grace, as were Maureen's too regal nose and Theresa's pointy chin. Each had been given a protection against vanity, a weapon against pride. Among them all, only Johnny had been denied some saving flaw. To Dempsey, all the genetic experiments practiced upon the sisters finally found their proper combination in him. Previous errors were corrected; failed trials were rectified. Faults and flaws in his sisters had rearranged themselves in Johnny. Johnny had been given the final reshaping, previous imbalances had been brought in line, new symmetries devised. He defined perfection. And this, Dempsey acknowledged, was what it meant to be in love.

By now the bracelet had exhausted the attention it deserved and, led by Maureen, the sisters descended on Dempsey. Now there were more protracted introductions, handshakes from Patricia and Maureen, a quick kiss from Theresa. It occurred to Dempsey—fleetingly—that her view of the sisters had been distorted. They were, each in her own way, rather beautiful. It was her own standards that may have been awry.

Now Johnny's arm was around her waist, his nose in her ear, a coupling permissible under the circumstances. The sisters, with their earlier advance upon Dempsey, had merely prepared the way for Johnny's mother, who had been the last to greet her. She was a fair-sized woman about five and a half feet tall. She had a long narrow face and a long narrow nose. Her eyes were blue and bright and her chin slightly recessive. (Apparently she'd saved her chin allotment for Johnny and for Patricia, cutting Theresa out of the deal completely.) But her hair she'd obviously decided to keep for herself. It was black and shiny. All of her children had been denied even a hint of such sleek fine hair, and Dempsey thought she saw, in the woman's smile, a secret pleasure, a sly satisfaction, that she'd managed to keep this one splendor for herself.

"I wanted to come down to the ferry," the woman had said, "but Patricia didn't make the salad she promised and—well—you understand." She now took Dempsey by the arm and was leading her away from her children, toward some chairs grouped toward the back of the yard. "And the bracelet's a honey. A real honey. It'll fit right in with my collection."

Dempsey wanted to stop in her tracks, but the pull of the woman's arm kept her on course toward the chairs. What had made her think that she was being original in giving a woman named Rose a bracelet with a rose on it? In a near whisper, as if this were a confidence, Mrs. Donegan continued: "I have the most extraordinary—extra *ordinary*—collection of jewelry with roses—earrings, bracelets, rings, brooches, pins, necklaces—you name it. Hat pins you put in your hair even if you don't wear a hat. I've got 'em all. I'll show it to you some time, the collection. Not today. It'd take the whole afternoon." Mrs. Donegan held up her arm and wriggled the new bracelet, rattling it against another not completely unlike it.

They had reached the chairs, but just when Dempsey was half-lowered onto a seat, Mrs. Donegan said, "Oh!

Wait!" Mrs. Donegan had decided Dempsey must first have a tour of the yard. Dempsey got up. There was a side yard and a backyard. The side yard was for grass bordered by flowers, hyacinths and tulips now gone, but irises and tiger lilies and sweet william in full bloom. (Dempsey knew the names from her still-life classes.) The backyard was for vegetables and it had a toolshed. Between them was a grape arbor, which could also be used as a shaded patio if the sun was too hot. Dempsey, without asking, ate one of the grapes. It was bitter, like a currant. "Jack, my husband," Mrs. Donegan told her, "made wine as if he were Italian. Every year. The press is in the toolshed if you want to see it. No one drank the wine except Jack. Killed him, I'm convinced of it."

Dempsey noticed a wobble in the woman's walk. Mrs. Donegan was wearing pumps with spiked heels. The heels would catch in some of the softer ground and puncture some of the soil as they went.

Next, Dempsey was shown the tomatoes, the beets, the onions and radishes, the lettuce and kale, the poked holes from the high heels pocking the ground wherever they went. When they'd finished, at the six stalks of corn along the back fence, the garden looked as if it had been visited by a pestilence of burrowing rodents that could even now be feasting on beets and onions, on carrots and all the roots that lay beneath the punctured ground.

They returned to the lawn chairs but, again, before Dempsey could settle herself down into her seat, Mrs. Donegan detained her. "No! Wait! Here's Andrew with the baby." Once more Dempsey pulled herself upright. There at the side door of the house was a large man and a child. Johnny hadn't told her anything about the boy who was holding a toy, a plastic bubble the size of a melon, at the end of a stick. There were wheels alongside the bubble and Dempsey could see what looked like colored Ping-Pong balls inside. The hand not holding the toy was covering the child's eyes.

Dempsey stared at the child, unable to blink. Like Doctor Norstar's Joey, the boy was the age, the size her son would now be. She had been curious about what Johnny's family was like. Now she would find out in a way she had not prepared herself for.

Like maiden aunts for whom a nephew is the center of the universe, Patricia and Maureen went fluttering and clucking toward the doorway as if they were not, respectively, the mother of a son and daughter and the mother of two daughters. They approached the man and child with cries and cackles, "Terry, so adorable," anticipating the joy now made possible. Theresa, because she was the boy's mother, stayed where she was, Johnny at her side, examining the irises planted along the sidewalk fence. Mrs. Donegan moved swiftly through the grass, determined to beat her daughters to the prize, but her spiked heels allowed Patricia and Maureen to make it to the finish line while their mother was still busy poking holes in the turf.

When Mrs. Donegan finally arrived, however, her precedence was immediately acknowledged. Terry, who had been passed from his father to Patricia to Maureen, squeezed, hugged, and given enough kisses on the top of his head to raise the soft blond hair into an irremediable tangle, was now handed on to his grandmother. Having cast herself as rescuer, Mrs. Donegan turned away from the agitated aunts, holding a long kiss on the child's cheek. It was as if she had saved the boy from being mauled by the furies and must now reassure him that he was safe in Grandma's arms.

The boy looked back at his father, who was still

standing at the side door, then toward his mother, bent over the irises. The child seemed to be asking why this was happening to him. No answer was forthcoming.

Dempsey was transfixed. Difficult as it was, she couldn't take her eyes off the boy, but she must. She had to blink, to smile. But please, she needed help. This time it was Andrew to the rescue.

"I'm Andrew. You're Dempsey." He held out his hand.

The handshake was quick, once down, once up, and that was it, but the man's clasp was firm without insisting that it be impressive. He wasn't, as Dempsey had first thought, fat; he was just big. Robust. But with a baby face, pink, full-cheeked, with thin blond hair much like his son's. The eyes were blue, though too pale to give them any prominence. It seemed he was trying not to be shy, looking directly at Dempsey, but not sure what he should do next. For a moment she thought he was about to turn and walk away, the protocols having been observed, but Johnny thoughtfully came up and intervened by putting his hand on his brother-in-law's shoulder, forcing him to stay where he was.

"This is Andrew."

"We've met," Dempsey managed a feeble smile to indicate that it has been pleasant. Andrew nodded.

"Andrew works in Jersey," Johnny said.

"Oh? Really?" She hoped that this sounded as if she wanted him to expand on the subject. But this time it was Mrs. Donegan who intervened.

"This is Andrew," she said.

"Yes." Dempsey smiled again, not quite as weakly as before.

"You're a painter," Andrew said. "An artist."

Dempsey was able to laugh feebly. "I'm afraid so."

"Don't be afraid," Andrew said. "Somebody's got to do it. We need art or what good are we?"

Dempsey wanted to say something meaningful, but nothing presented itself. So Andrew continued, "I wanted to be a painter, an artist. But I was too afraid."

Dempsey was genuinely puzzled. "Afraid? Of what?"

"Don't listen to him," Mrs. Donegan said. "Andrew's not afraid of anything."

"I was afraid because I didn't know where it might take me, being a painter, being an artist. It was like going into the woods at night. I was always afraid of what might be there. I still am."

Before Dempsey told him she thought this was a legitimate concern, Mrs. Donegan laughed and said, "You are not afraid of something so silly. Now Andrew, come on."

Dempsey smiled demurely. "Actually, what he says makes sense to me. In fact, I couldn't have said it any better myself."

Without taking his eyes off Dempsey, Andrew reached out and took hold of her hand. "Ah yes, thank for your understanding. But that's because you're an artist," he said. "And I'm so pleased to meet you." He lifted the hand to his lips and kissed it, held it there a moment, then lowered it. He looked away. As if the moment had never happened, he shouted to his son, his voice clear and joyful, "Terry! Show Daddy how high you can jump!" Terry, catching the cue, came running across the grass, squealing, picking up speed as he came, his arms outstretched. He leapt forward, throwing himself toward his father. Andrew caught him in his huge hands and, with one wide sweeping gesture, lifted the boy high above him—the feet raised higher, the head aimed down toward his father, the two of them screaming in triumph.

Andrew tilted the boy's body from side to side; the boy kicked his feet into the air. Together they screamed once more. "See how high you can jump! See how high!" Again the body was tilted and the feet kicked; again the screams came forth. There was, of course, applause and Dempsey was determined to participate fully in what was going on.

Now everyone was finally allowed to sit on the lawn chairs. There was picnic food. Andrew was at the grill. Arranged on the table at the side of the house there was Italian sausage, potato salad, large unpitted olives, fresh tomatoes, scallions from the garden, deviled eggs, and pickles. There was Pepsi and beer. There would be Patricia's pound cake with ice cream. There would be strawberries and watermelon.

Dempsey, for this occasion, ate slowly, asking each bite if it intended to give her any trouble. She avoided pickles but was willing to take her chances with the sausage. Italian sausage was an old, long-neglected weakness and she wouldn't refuse it now. If there was real trouble, she had extra underclothes in her tote bag and she was wearing a shield in her panties.

But now there was talk. Plenty of talk. Family talk. This was what she had come for, and it was a persisting challenge not to keep staring at the boy with her own sorrow that, she knew, she must do all in her power to suppress.

Johnny, his hand holding Dempsey's hand on the arm of his chair, was telling her about his childhood chore as bottle washer for his father's wine. "It was the most boring job I ever had. Washing out wine bottles every fall. My dad wasn't all that good about getting the sediment out of the wine and it'd stick inside even if he rinsed the bottles right away."

Terry, meanwhile, was wheeling his toy around the grass, the colored balls inside the bubble ricocheting off the plastic like popcorn popping. He was "mowing the lawn," and was interrupted frequently with praise and encouragement.

At one point, however, Terry came up and put his hand on his uncle's knee. Johnny let go of Dempsey's hand and placed it on the boy's head, touseled his light brown hair, then said,

I never saw a purple cow
I never hope to see one
But I will tell you anyhow
I'd rather see than be one.

Terry took a moment to process the information, considering it as seriously as his uncle had presented it. Dempsey kept herself from reaching out and touching the boy's cheek with a loving hand, afraid of growing tearful.

Fortunately, Terry returned to his toy and Dempsey realized that Maureen was talking to her.

"See that catalpa tree near the back fence, where you can tell that a lower branch has been sawed off?" she was saying. "Johnny, do you want to tell Dempsey or should I?"

Johnny with a sly smile said, "I don't know what you're talking about."

Theresa jumped in. "Maureen, you tell her."

"Well, if you insist."

"I insist."

"All right then." She tapped Dempsey's arm, then said, "Well, your friend, John Francis Donegan, when he was fourteen —"

"Thirteen," Johnny said.

"All right then. Thirteen. And after being almost the

shortest kid in his class, all of a sudden began to shoot up like a beanstalk. One day he goes to collect some of the catalpa seedpods—we call them Indian cigars—and wham, he bonks his head on a lower branch. And what does he do? Instead of just ducking the next time, he saws off the branch. And does he stop with that? Oh no. Not John Francis. He builds a bonfire to burn the branch and almost sets fire to the back fence."

Dempsey, to her relief, had finally entered into the spirit of the gathering, which prompted her to say, "Is that why he became a fireman?"

Patricia clapped her hands. "Dempsey! Dempsey! You got it! You got it!"

Theresa laughed and said, "Johnny, where did you find her?"

Mrs. Donegan shook her head with pleased amazement and kept repeating, "Dempsey! Dempsey! Dempsey!"

The raucous response to her triumphant comment began to calm itself. Dempsey, as if rewarding herself for the successful one-liner, allowed herself to check on Terry. There he was at the food table, stuffing a deviled egg into his mouth and, while he was chewing, he began to play with the olives in the bowl next to the pickles. As he was swallowing the egg, he tipped the olive bowl toward himself, picked one out, and popped it into his mouth.

Dempsey then saw him reach for another olive, then pull back his hand. She looked sadly at his pudgy legs, the tan shorts and the shirt with teddy bears crawling all over it. His back was to her and she noticed he was bringing his slender shoulders up, then up farther as if trying to make himself taller. His head was sinking slowly between his shoulders, the shoulders themselves jerking upward.

Dempsey let her plate fall to her feet, dumping her food onto Johnny's shoe. She sprang toward the boy, spun him around and saw the terrified look on his face, the bugged eyes, the dampening skin. She grabbed him by the ankles with one hand and put the other under his head so it wouldn't hit the ground. She yanked him upward and turned him upside down. One ankle broke free from her grip. There was no time to retrieve it. She whacked the boy on the back between his shoulders, then whacked him again, and then again, lifting him higher each time so her hand wouldn't have to go too far away before she could whack him once more. Desperate to hear the cry, the wail that would tell her he was still alive, she started to bring her hand toward the child's back one more time, but there was a curling of his body, then a stretch straight down toward the ground. The loud cry came, a wailing that seemed to have started in a far place and had only now arrived. Dempsey held him by the one ankle and breathed deeply.

And now they were upon her. "What's she doing? Stop! She's gone crazy. Quick, grab her. Does she always get like this? Get him away from her. Johnny, how could you bring —" Johnny had taken Dempsey by the shoulder and yanked her away from the others. The boy was now in his grandmother's arms. His father, roasting fork in hand, was coming toward them.

Johnny stared up into Dempsey's face. He was trying to say something, but couldn't. His hand began to rise. Was he going to hit her? But the hand was lowered. His mouth began to open. He was going to say something. Again the hand started to rise.

"An olive," Dempsey said, the words more rasped than spoken. She had no breath left. She was sure that she would, at that moment, soil herself. She would throw up, she would lose her mind. She dropped to her knees, kneeling on the grass. "The olive was choking him."

"What the—?" Johnny bent over her and took her by the arm. She pulled herself free. As if she had gone blind, Dempsey frantically patted the grass in front of her, then out away from her, then back again. She found nothing. She started again, this time patting harder, reaching farther, whimpering, begging to find what she was looking for.

"Dempsey—" Johnny was determined to help her up. Again she pulled away. When she felt the olive beneath her hand, she let her head fall farther forward, her hair touching the grass. Johnny had squatted in front of her and was trying to lift her by both shoulders. She let herself be helped to stand.

With the side of her hand, she brushed the hair from her face. Johnny hadn't let go of her shoulders, but Dempsey could see Mrs. Donegan, the others, arrayed a few feet in front of her. They were saying nothing. Terry was in his father's arms. His father was staring at Dempsey. They all were.

So small the object seemed, so pitiful a justification. But she held it up anyway for them to see. Terry turned his face toward his father's chest. "Olive," Dempsey whispered. "Choking. He was choking." She turned to Johnny. "Maybe I should have let you, you'd know better what to do, but there wasn't time." She held her hand out to Mrs. Donegan. "Here." She put the olive into the woman's hand, gently, so they wouldn't crunch the frail bones or break through the taut skin. It took everyone a moment to identify it as an olive. Dempsey wet her shield.

When the ferry had moved out no more than fifty feet from the slip, Dempsey saw that a mist was rising from the water. It had gotten colder and, as if to hide rather than to end the summer day, a fog was obscuring the island and all the people on it. Johnny, who had duty at eleven and hadn't slept all afternoon, was stretched out on a bench, Dempsey's tote pillowing his head. He'd promised to close his eyes. She'd promised to wake him when they passed the Statue of Liberty.

Revealed to the Donegans as a savior, placing herself in the tradition of rescuer, Dempsey was accepted as an equal and given hints, by gesture and intonation, that she was considered a promising initiate destined, perhaps, to become one of them. At parting, Patricia and Maureen had kissed her; Theresa insisted Terry shake her hand; Andrew touched her shoulder. "Thank you for saving my boy," he said. And Mrs. Donegan had given her a hatpin crowned with a rose.

Dempsey had not gotten sick.

So dense had the fog become that foghorns were calling plaintively to each other from distant waters as if trying to set the pitch for the song the whales would sing. A buoy marking the channel was rocking in the advancing waves, its bell tolling an hour beyond anyone's counting.

Dempsey gazed into the unmoving mist. With each blink she caught the image indelibly slapped onto the surface of her eyes and smacked into the back of her brain: the moment before she had shown the olive in proof of her innocence. Still on her knees, she had raised her head and had seen, arrayed against her, not only Johnny's family but Johnny himself, all the fierce, horrified condemnation locked into the set of their bones, frozen into the stare of their widened eyes. For that one sharp moment she had accepted, even approved, of the way they were seeing her.

A devastating truth was revealed: she saved the boy,

but she had not saved her own son. She had given him AIDS and nothing could save him. She was deserving of any scorn that was heaped upon her. Also, in that moment, she accepted and approved of what awaited her, not just her death but a death brought on by any number of the horrors included in the AIDS repertory. And to her as well came a truth she had managed to suppress: her refusal to take her medicines, her insistence to herself that she was playing a game with her illness. It was all a fraud. She'd been inviting the sickness to do its worst. She would welcome it. She deserved it. She had given her son not life, but death—and now her own death should be a horror beyond imagining.

The buoy sounded its knell, but farther away. Dempsey had brought her arms up and was about to fold them across her chest, but she lowered them instead, surrendering to the fog whispering around her.

7.

Doctor Norstar sat on the edge of the overstuffed chair in her waiting room and read from the folder in her hand. She put the folder on the table next to the couch and pinched the bridge of her nose. After she'd taken her fingers away, she opened her eyes, then picked up the folder again and continued her reading. Dempsey, sitting on the couch, straightened up, then slumped back down, trying to relax. She considered reaching down into her bag and taking out her knitting, but Doctor Norstar kept looking as if she were about to say something, even though she continued to say nothing at all.

A workman, one of the two movers, walked by carrying a carton shaped like a file drawer. Maybe it was a file drawer. He put it near the elevator, then went back down the hallway toward Doctor Norstar's office. A second mover, younger, passed by wheeling a chair. (While Doctor Norstar's chair had wheels, the patient's chair was planted firmly onto the floor, aimed at Doctor Norstar. The doctor had been free to swivel and roll at will, escaping the patient's gaze, while the patient was made to keep all eyes on the doctor and to sit still.)

Today was moving day for Doctor Norstar. It was after office hours, but she had phoned Dempsey and had told her to come anyway, as long as she did not mind the mess and the distractions. The office was being moved to larger quarters upstairs in the same building, quarters Doctor Norstar would share with Doctor Willens. Doctor Willens looked after Doctor Norstar's patients when she wasn't available—and she looked after his in similar circumstance. The two of them were practicing in similar areas and doing research that was always being compared and discussed, so they'd decided to combine forces more completely and, in the process, share the rent.

The tone of Doctor Norstar's voice when she'd called had let Dempsey know something was going on, and the doctor's directive to come that day after the office had closed had confirmed the impression of urgency. The doctor would say no more until they'd met. The implication was that something terrible was happening, or about to happen, and Dempsey must be told. That was why the doctor had sent for her; she had to be given the news in person. Dempsey had been expecting this. There had been a flurry of activity these past few weeks. The bloodletting had had to be repeated because of continuing errors in the lab. Twice she had gone back to the clinic and given more blood. From the blood and the urine, the doctor, almost in a panic, had gone to vaginal smears, then, of all things, saliva. When asked again the reasons behind all these inconveniences, the doctor would only say, "Something's wrong. I have to find out what it is. As soon as I know, I'll tell you. Try if you can to stop asking." She then ordered samples extracted from the lymph nodes. Then a spinal tap that would give specimens of cerebral fluid. (None of this had Dempsey mentioned to Johnny. He would only become more impatient and anxious than she. All appointments were deliberately scheduled for those hours when he'd be on duty, and Dr. Norstar had complied. Dempsey would find out what was happening, then tell him. Maybe.)

By now, Dempsey had managed to feel an even greater sympathy for Doctor Norstar. At times the woman seemed more confused, more exhausted than Dempsey herself. The phrase *polymerase chain reaction* was mentioned. Retrovirology lab was also mentioned as well as amplified DNA. Doctor Norstar was searching for something, something that frightened her. But when Dempsey, as casually as she could, asked for explanations, the doctor would beg her not to ask—just yet. Nothing could be said. Dempsey wondered if she had been selected for experiments that would locate and possibly correct some appalling flaw in medical procedures. She had not volunteered, but neither had she refused. She liked Doctor Norstar; she felt she owed her something for not having taken the medicines the doctor had prescribed. It had occurred to Dempsey that the testing bore some relation to the absence of medication in her system. Then considered that she was being punished for her refusals, for her obstinacy. Doctor Norstar would keep testing her, continue draining her blood, collecting her urine, her saliva, subjecting her to vaginal probes and spinal inflictions, until she would finally admit she hadn't been taking her medicine.

At some moments, Dempsey feared that a new strain of the virus had surfaced in her system, an even more insidious mutation of the already fatal infection. This would account for the doctor's fearful reluctance to report her findings. At other times, Dempsey would scoff at the doctor's concern. There could hardly be much that the virus—or its mutant—could do to her that wasn't already being accomplished. She was already receptive to any microbe that might cross her path. She was already gathering to herself more ailments than she would be given time to handle. No infection was turned away unaccommodated, no bacterium was refused her readied hospitality.

After the phone call earlier that day, Dempsey had been relieved, then jittery, then resigned, then angry for what she was being put through. If she could just hang on to her anger, she'd be all right. If she was furious enough, she could be told anything. She must concentrate on her grievances, the pains, the indignities, the pricks and pokes and stabbings—all practiced on her hapless, unasking person. She must dwell on the stupidities, the misjudgments, the indifference, the hidden crimes of the medical profession. She must prepare the speech she'd make to Doctor Norstar. She must rehearse the invective, she must heighten the indignation. The speech must be ready for immediate delivery, the withering response that would reduce Doctor Norstar to a state of suppliant apology. Doctor Norstar must be made to pay for her failures, for her ineptitude, her ignorance. That all the testing would result in no particular treatment made no difference. Ultimately, whatever would be prescribed or suggested would be refused.

And yet Dempsey still demanded of Doctor Norstar that she be prescient and informed. Dempsey had continued coming to her even after she had stopped taking the medicines because the doctor's interest in her condition remained independent of the treatments the condition might require. Doctor Norstar had become, for Dempsey, something of a psychic, a fortune-teller. She would predict what was yet to come; she could provide specifics that would help Dempsey prepare for what lay ahead. So it was this withdrawal of prediction that enraged her now. That the psychic should lose her powers was not permissible, that her prophecies should be withheld was not allowed.

When Dempsey, walking briskly up Sixth Avenue

to Doctor Norstar's office that afternoon, had come to Houston Street and was waiting for the light to change, she found her mind's eye glaring down at a cowering Doctor Norstar, she decided she'd just wait and hear what the good doctor had to say and determine then what she might do in response. To simply nod in recognition and acceptance of the doctor's words would probably be the most appropriate thing to do.

The first mover passed again, this time carrying a painting of what appeared to be flowers, but flowers of the artist's own creation, exploded orchids showing great bursts of orange and blue, a carnage of color blaring out from behind the glass. Dempsey had looked at it—and the other paintings in the doctor's office—for longer periods of time than she'd given to most paintings by other artists. Directly behind Doctor Norstar's desk—a point of refuge for anyone not wanting to look directly at the doctor—had been another painting by the same artist—this one not an explosion outward, but—in greens and blues—a screen of leaf-shaped flowers that seemed to invite the viewer to enter and be refreshed, to wander and be at peace. Dempsey had assumed that Doctor Norstar had a good eye and the requisite spirit to choose her office decor wisely, but when she'd asked about the paintings on an earlier visit, the doctor all but dismissed them. They had been painted by one of her patients and accepted in place of payment. The doctor had deliberately put them in the office so the artist could see them up there on the wall. He'd painted them because he was dying. Then he'd died. She'd left them where they were because she'd forgotten they were there.

After Dempsey learned about the artist, she avoided looking at the paintings. She considered them a rebuke, their insistence on the flourishing and the beautiful. The artist had chosen to bless when he'd been given an opportunity to curse. The paintings had a charity that the artist could have resisted. But he hadn't. In Doctor Norstar's office Dempsey would turn away from the paintings toward the airshaft window, where she could give her full attention to the gray brick wall five feet away.

After reviewing several pages and charts in the folder, Doctor Norstar began shuffling faster. Then she started again at the beginning, again increasing her speed the deeper she got into the file. Both movers went past now, carrying a metal cabinet. Doctor Norstar put her fist on the file. "Wait here a minute," she said. "I need another folder. I hope they didn't take it upstairs." She put the folder on the table next to the couch again—the coffee table had already been removed—and went down the hall into her office. Dempsey saw her name on the tab sticking out of the file, "Coates, Dempsey." She was tempted to take the folder, open it, and try to discover what all the fuss was about. It would tell her what was happening. She could prepare herself for what Doctor Norstar was about to say. It was, after all, her file.

Did the pages hold only facts or were there impressions as well? What did Doctor Norstar really think of her? "Patient looks lousy." "Patient intelligent but uncooperative." The folder would tell her and then she'd know. "Ms. Coates has strong hair; Ms. Coates has hands of construction worker." Or did it say, "Dempsey?" "Dempsey out of denial. Dempsey into anger." Perhaps the notes began with "patient," then moved on to "Ms. Coates" and finally to "Dempsey." The folder would allow her not only to trace her ups and downs but also to follow the pattern of the doctor's experience regarding her, the patient, Dempsey Coates.

Just as Dempsey had convinced herself that Doctor Norstar wouldn't mind if she checked her own file, that the doctor had, in fact, left it there deliberately so she could sneak a look, Doctor Norstar came out with the other folder. She sat down and opened it, turned two pages, then said," "Now." The word, as intended, brought Dempsey up to the present. The past was dismissed; it was of no importance except as prelude to the moment about to take place. As preface, the word emphasized the gravity of what was about to be spoken.

"Drug abuser," Doctor Norstar said quietly, looking at the page in front of her. "Heroin, less than six months' addiction, pregnancy, impregnator unknown, drug abuse ended within first term of pregnancy, no assistance in withdrawal, male child in sixth month, two-pounds-three-ounces, lived six hours, cause of death —"

"I know all this," Dempsey said. "If you want to make sure I'm Dempsey Coates, I admit it. I confess. I am Dempsey Coates. I did all those things. Now can we skip to today?"

Doctor Norstar, not looking up, pulled her upper lip in between her teeth, then released it so she could bite her lower lip. That, too, was then released. "This is for my benefit, this review, not for yours. I have more than one patient, although I do my best to conceal the fact. I need to repeat to myself the patient's history specifically, going over it step by step whenever an important change takes place. That's why I needed the folder. Try to understand."

"All right. I understand," Dempsey said. "Male child dead. Cause of death: AIDS congenitally contracted from mother, from Dempsey Coates, drug abuser, needle user—See? Now you know it all. So tell me, why am I here? Whatever you have to say, I'm ready. So just say it and let's get it over with."

The two movers went by, carrying, not without difficulty, Doctor Norstar's desk. The doctor's office would be empty by now. But the second painting—the blues and greens, the peaceful lure, had not gone by. Maybe it had been removed earlier, before she'd arrived.

"Let me ask you this," Doctor Norstar said. She paused, thought a moment, then looked at Dempsey. "Have you been getting any. . . alternative treatment?"

"No. None."

"Herbs, medicines from other countries not approved yet? Acupuncture even. Or meditation? Anything?"

"I don't even take the medicine you've given me— "

"Oh?"

"But never mind. Please, please go on."

"I'll repeat the question. Have you been trying anything else?"

"Not that I know of."

"Dempsey, please!— "

"All right, all right. No. Why? Do you think I'm back on drugs?"

"Are you?"

"No."

"You're not receiving any substance beyond food and drink?"

"I don't pay much attention to diet, if that's what you want to know. Pizza, an occasional cheeseburger, a particular fondness for strawberries."

"All right, all right." The doctor looked down again at the folder on her lap. "AIDS diagnosis after pneumonia, history of night sweats previous to diagnosis. MAI thought to be digestive problem, thrush— "

"I'm going mad, perhaps?" Dempsey said quietly.

"Just be patient, please. I have to review your history—

for my own sake. I can't just say what I'm going to say."

"Yes, you can. Go ahead and say it."

"Now just stop!"

Dempsey settled back onto the couch. "Well, whenever you're ready."

The doctor looked directly at her. "You're cured," she said.

Neither moved. They continued to look directly at each other. "I couldn't mention even the possibility until I was sure," the doctor said. "It would have been unfair, to say the least. It would have been the worst cruelty ever inflicted on a patient—if I'd made you hope and then . . . At first it was the T-cells, the count too high: it couldn't be. I knew it couldn't be. Then the test for antibodies: It was negative. Negative. It couldn't be negative. It can't go from positive to negative. But it did. The virus was there, I knew it was there. I had to find it. It was hiding, but it was there—someplace. PCR—that's why I had it done—Polymerase Chain Reaction. Amplified DNA. The virus had to be there. Somewhere. Anywhere. Urine, saliva, spinal fluid. Where was it? Where had it gone? This is not a benign virus we're talking about. It has disguises, it has tricks. It mocks, it deceives. But it's always there, somewhere, waiting patiently: but for you, it's not there. Not anymore. It's gone. You're cured."

The word *cured,* like the first time she'd heard the word *AIDS,* reached Dempsey's ear from a distant place. It had not yet become the word itself. She could hear it. She could even blink her eyes. She might even nod her head, acknowledging the sound itself: cure. But it still wasn't a word.

Again the doctor said, "You're cured."

Dempsey nodded her head.

"The virus, it's gone. It's not there. We looked everywhere. It can't hide that effectively. We would have found it *somewhere*. Dead? Escaped? Who knows? We know nothing. Nothing at all. Except that all traces are gone, vanished. Even the immune system has reconstructed itself. How could that possibly be? A cure, if we ever find one, might stop the virus, but the immune system—what will happen to that, we have no idea. But yours—"

"Cured?" Dempsey said the word, trying to give it some reality. "Cured?"

"Who knows what the right word is. You do not have the virus. You don't even show any leftover signs of the lung and liver damage, any of the signs that should still be there no matter what. It's as though you were never infected, never been ill. All gone—without a trace. It has to be called a cure. Why not?" The doctor's voice had become more professional, the words clipped, precise.

The old indifference, Doctor Norstar's first line of defense against challenge or contradiction, brought coldness into her eyes. She lifted her head even higher. She'd arrived at the proud imperiousness that Dempsey recognized as her last defense. "In medical terms," the doctor said, "you're declared a cure."

Dempsey rubbed her forefinger along a streak of paint on her jeans—Davy's Gray, the paint was called. She scratched it with her fingernail, then rubbed it again, but more gently than before as if apologizing to her jeans for the scratching. "You're sure?" she asked.

"I wouldn't have dared mention it—even hint at it—if I weren't sure. Yes. I'm sure. It's been verified. A whole team of us. A team, a horde, an army—"

"But how?"

"*You* tell *me*. Maybe I'm the one demented, but I even caught myself thinking: Dempsey will know. Dempsey will tell me. Tell all of us. Well? Do you know? Can you tell me?"

"How can I tell you anything when I don't know what you're talking about?"

"You don't have AIDS. You have no antibodies. You test negative. No AIDS. No HIV. Cured. Can you understand that?"

"No."

Doctor Norstar closed the folder and put her hand on top. "That's all right. Neither can I."

"Is that all you have to say?"

The doctor flinched. "I'm happy for you. We all are. You must come meet the team, hear what we have to say, how pleased—" She stopped and placed both hands on top of the file. She leaned down and gave all her weight to the closed folder. "No, we're not happy," she said. "We're furious. Why you?"

"I don't know."

"Of course you don't know. If there was anything to be known, we'd know it. We're not stupid—all evidence to the contrary. We do know *something*. We work, we slave, we grope, we crawl. We ache until we can't move, until we can't think. Until we've nothing left. Which means we're back at the beginning and we start all over again. And again. And then—you come along and we've done nothing, no one's done anything—and you're cured. Now can you hear me? Cured, Goddamn it. Cured. *Now* do you know what I'm talking about? *Now* do you understand?"

"No."

"Then don't."

Doctor Norstar waited. She put her hand to her cheek as if to check for a fever. After she'd taken the hand away, she said quite gently, "Do you ever pray? Did you ever pray that—" She stopped. "No! Don't answer that. It's nothing I want even to come near. Forget I asked. I *didn't* ask. That has nothing to do with me. Forget I even mentioned it."

The elevator door opened and the two men came out, marching almost in lockstep, one behind the other, their arms swinging in measured arcs as if they'd been sent by some higher authority to perform an important official act. They broke step as the older one came and stood in front of Dempsey, facing Doctor Norstar. "We have to take the couch now," he said.

"And the chair and table," the other man added.

"Yeah. And the chair and table."

"Then we're finished on time," the younger man said.

"Yeah. Five minutes into the next hour and you have to pay the whole hour. We want to save you."

Doctor Norstar stood up. Dempsey stood up. They moved free of the couch, the chair, the table. The doctor had the folder in her hand.

The older man carried the chair, the younger man came back for the table. Doctor Norstar moved toward the counter where Daphne, the receptionist, had worked. At one end, near the wall, there was a paper clip. The doctor picked it up, rubbed it with her fingers. "I'm sorry," she said. "I shouldn't have become so impatient. Forgive me. I made a common mistake. As a doctor it's an occupational hazard to forget that I'm dealing with the human body. I should learn to expect anything." She put down the paper clip.

The men marched back into the room and stationed themselves one at each end of the couch. At a nod from the older man, they squatted and picked the couch up from underneath and lifted it, raising it no farther than a few feet from the floor. With short, prissy little steps they hauled the couch, like a final helpless corpse, to the elevator. "We should have done the couch first," the younger man said.

"Shut up and get in," the older man said.

The younger man got in, then the older man. The door closed. The office was empty except for Dempsey, Doctor Norstar, and the paper clip. Everything, everyone else had gone.

8.

As Dempsey walked down Hudson Street on her way home, she kept repeating, like a mantra, *cured, cured, cured*—trying to understand what it meant. Soon it would threaten her sanity. Maybe if she concentrated on things more specifically implied by the word she kept repeating, she might be able to grasp the reality of what she'd been told.

Her first choice of subject was that now she'd very definitely be able to finish the Lazarus paintings. Then what would she do? It appalled her to realize she'd made no plans beyond that. She'd given it no thought. Now she told herself to come up with a few possibilities before she crossed Horatio Street. She decided to move on to an even more unexplored subject.

She would, of course, marry Johnny. And then—? And then they'd have a long life together. And then—? There would be children. She tried to rush past the subject, but that was not to be allowed. Then the children would live. She'd be a mother, Johnny, a father. But what did that mean?

No actual scenes presented themselves to her imagination. She tried, but the only image she could summon was of the men carrying the couch into the elevator. When she came to Christopher Street, she considered just standing there, refusing to cross until she could visualize some event made possible by this inexplicable bewilderment. But before she could come to an image, she heard a voice, rasping and high-pitched, call out, "Dempsey!"

Tom Van Tyl was coming toward her. Slowly, very slowly. He was wearing a heavy woolen Irish sweater. Around his neck was a gray-and-black cashmere scarf and on his head a black-knitted cap pulled halfway down over his ears. It took Dempsey a few seconds to decipher the strangeness of what she saw. The day was warm with only the softest breeze coming up from the river. It took fewer seconds for Dempsey to connect this unseasonable garb with a known fact. Tom had AIDS, and the last she'd heard, he had closed the gallery on Wooster Street that he and his companion Michael—already dead—had run for more than seventeen years. Tom would be subject to chills or, quite possibly, he was feeling the final chill that had become unrelenting.

"Tom!"

Now she could see his face, the lesions caused by an all-too-common affliction, Kaposi's sarcoma, that had disfigured his once-handsome face. She quickly said the obligatory, "You look great!"

Tom could only grunt. He was out of breath. He did manage to say, "Tell that to my doctor. He keeps telling me my T-cells are dropping like a January thermometer. The way he talks, you'd think they were close to ten below."

To enjoy Dempsey's response to his witticism, he looked directly into her eyes. His own eyes were so needful that, with effort, Dempsey tapped his upper right arm and let out a near-credible laugh. "Tom! You still make me laugh."

Tom chose to shrug. "Why not? What are we supposed to do, cry?"

Dempsey shook her head and in an attempt to imply that his gift for humor was beyond belief, she said, "Tom. Tom."

Tom, too, shook his head. "Forgive me, but I have to run. I want to make it to the Christopher Street Pier before it gets too cold." No longer looking into her eyes, he said, "With my T-cells disappearing the way they are, I might not be able to get there as often as I'd like to. If at all." He turned aside and looked down. "Michael and I met on the Pier." He paused, then said, "I like to go there and spend some time with him." Again he paused as if lost in thought. Dempsey knew she should say something but didn't know what it was. Tom rescued her by finally saying, "I'd better run."

He then turned and, with effort, again took up the arduous task he'd set for himself.

Dempsey stayed where she was and watched his slow advance. She was completely immobilized. She waited and she watched until he was halfway to Greenwich Street.

A sudden impulse had taken hold of her—she had been cured—and now she wanted to tell him a cure was obviously possible. She was the proof. Couldn't he, too, be cured? He would be able to spend time with Michael on the Pier whenever he wanted to. If she could be cured, why not him? Without thinking further, she called out, "Tom! Wait!"

Tom stopped and turned around. His feeble response was, "I have to run."

Dempsey had almost caught up with him by the time he'd finished the sentence. She would let her own words proceed her. She would call out, "I had it too and I've just been cured!" But then she was close enough to see his face, the scattered lesions, the empty eyes, the sorrowing look.

She stopped. *What if I wasn't cured?* Was she ready to give him a vain hope, to drive him to an even deeper despair?

In a breathless gasp, he said, "What —?"

Dempsey opened her mouth.

After a moment, Tom gasped out the word again. "What —?"

Dempsey pulled back a little and forced herself to say, "I —, I —, I just wanted to tell you to tell Michael I said, 'Hi!'" So feeble. So stupid. She couldn't possibly have been more inadequate.

But Tom slowly raised his right hand and put it gently on her cheek. Tears were welling up in his eyes. Still gasping, he said, "Oh, I will. I'll tell him. I promise I will. And — and — thank — thank you."

In a near whisper, Dempsey said, "It's all right. It's all right. Run along now. Michael's waiting."

Tom let out a long breath, moved his lips in an effort to smile, then turned around. He moved his torso forward three times, then took a first step. Then a second. Dempsey stayed where she was. She would wait until he had reached the pier. And as she watched and she waited, the word *cured* came to her in a completely different context than it had before. The only words that came to her now were: *Why me and not him? And why not Michael?*

Tom had reached the pier. Dempsey slowly turned and started back to Hudson Street. It was immediately apparent that she had been given a new refrain, one that again she must repeat over and over again. *Why me and not him? Why me and not* them? The one difference between this experience and the one before was that it was accompanied by a persisting image: Tom, enfeebled, walking out onto the Christopher Street Pier.

9.

There were fewer passengers on the upper deck, and Johnny was able to find an empty bench in the forward area. No one was directly behind him, and only one man three benches in front. The man was reading a magazine, a reasonable assurance that he'd continue reading for the entire trip and not feel he had a right to talk to Johnny because Johnny was wearing his fireman sweatshirt. People never bothered cops; priests and firemen were always fair game for anyone who wanted someone to listen. Johnny, when he'd left the loft, had forgotten what he was wearing; he should have been more attentive. But he wasn't.

He settled onto the seat, squirming a little—as if a bench on the Staten Island Ferry could somehow be made more comfortable if one just made the effort. He listened carefully for sounds. There was only the low growl of the motor and, far in the back, the low-pitched conversation between two teenaged girls, both of them Asian.

Johnny opened his manual. The exam was still over a month away, but he considered himself a slow study and applied the maxim drilled into him by his high school English teacher: *Repetitio mater studiorum est.* Repetition is the mother of study. Well, he would *repetitio* and *repetitio* and hope some of the *repetitio*s made it through his skull and into his brain.

Ordinarily he would go out on deck and look at the

Brooklyn Bridge until the ferry had veered to the right toward the Statue of Liberty and Ellis Island. Then he would cross to the other side and look at EIlis Island. After that he would have a hot dog. Then he would move forward and watch the home island come closer and closer, stealthy in its approach, but harmless. But now he was supposed to study. He had promised himself he would study and he must not break his promise.

He opened the manual to the section on ladders. He had already gone through the subject—more than twice—but it wouldn't hurt to do it again. *When a thirty-foot ladder is being raised to the roof, the point for tying the clove hitch is the twelfth rung from the top. To reach the eighth floor, a one-hundred-foot ladder, to reach the fourth floor, fifty feet or forty-five feet. The base of a fifty-foot trussed ladder should be placed twelve feet from the building. Set the axle jacks first when an aerial ladder is to go into service. A one-hundred-foot ladder can allow six men climbing . . .*

After he'd stared down at the page for at least two minutes and seen nothing, Johnny looked at the back of the head of the man reading the magazine. His hair was dark brown, long enough to touch his collar. His ears seemed tanned.

When Johnny had come into the loft earlier that evening, he hadn't, at first, seen Dempsey. She had taken one of the chairs away from the table and was sitting near the windows, off to the left near the ficus tree Johnny had planted in a bucket. The only colors in the loft were shades of gray. Nothing was blurred or misted over; most things were still distinguishably themselves—the paintings stacked faces to the wall, the worktable, the tin cans, bottles, jars, tubes, the kitchen area, the chairs, the ivy on the window ledge, the window shades drawn down to uneven lengths. The streetlight had not yet come on, and the single lit window across the street seemed to have held its light completely inside the pale yellow trapped by the glass, unable to spill into the air outside.

When Johnny had reached his hand over to the wall to turn on the light, he heard Dempsey's voice—soft, but without inflection. "Don't turn on the light. Please." There she was—a darker gray against the lighter gray of the windows. She was facing the room, angled slightly toward the kitchen cabinets. Her head was bowed, her hands resting on her lap.

"You're sitting in the dark." Dempsey said nothing. "You all right?"

"Yes, I'm all right."

"You want to go lie down?"

"No. I just want to sit here."

"In the dark?"

"It's not dark. I can see."

Dempsey turned her head to her right so she wouldn't be looking directly at him. "Maybe you could go for a walk, go someplace, and come back. Later."

Johnny went no closer. He pulled a chair away from the table, sat down and folded his hands in front of him. "You're feeling lousy, huh?"

"No. I'm feeling all right."

"Then why am I supposed to go out?"

"It's nice out. You could walk."

"You working? I mean, thinking?"

"No. I'm not working. I'm not thinking."

Johnny shoved the chair back and stood up. "I'm going to turn on the light."

"No. Don't. Please don't."

Johnny started around the table. "Your eyes. Are

your eyes bothering you? Is something happening to your eyes?"

"No. They're fine. They're all right."

"Are you sure?"

"Nothing is wrong with my eyes. Please. I'd like to just sit here for a little while. By myself. Is that all right, Johnny?" She sounded incredibly sad, resigned almost.

"I don't know. Is it?"

"Yes. It is. Honest it is." She turned her head toward him and said softly, "You go out. Walk. Anything. Come back when you see the lights on. It means—it will mean—it will mean the lights are on. And you can come back. All right?"

"I'm going to turn them on now. I've got to see what's happening."

"No, please don't!"

Dempsey was up from her chair. She rushed toward him and grabbed the back of his shirt. She immediately let go. The touch seemed to have frightened her. Johnny turned around. Dempsey stood, unmoving, her hands held up in front of her, palms outward.

"Okay," Johnny said quietly. "Maybe you're feeling sick. Maybe you'd rather be by yourself. But I'd like to help if I can." When she said nothing, he added, "Why won't you take some of the medicine? Please. I've begged you and begged you. And now I'm begging you again."

"Don't beg. There's no reason to beg."

"No? It's crazy not to take it. You know that? Crazy!"

"I'm not crazy." Her voice was even quieter than before. She went back to her chair and sat down, assuming the same pose she'd had when Johnny had come into the room. It was as if she wanted not to have gotten up; she wanted not to have grabbed his shirt. Johnny waited for her to repeat her dismissal, her request that he leave her alone. She said nothing. Johnny decided he wouldn't move until she told him to.

She lifted her head. "Do you pray for me?" she asked.

"Yes. Sometimes."

"What do you pray for?"

"For you. I pray for you."

"For what for me?"

"I don't understand."

"You ask for something. What do you ask for?"

"I don't know. I mean, it changes. When you're in pain, when you cough and it keeps getting worse. Or when you have to lie down all of a sudden and I'm afraid you're going to die, I pray."

"What?"

"That it stop. That you'll be all right."

Johnny could hear her breathing. And his own breathing. Then Dempsey said, "Did you ever pray that I would be cured?"

Johnny waited a moment, then said, "No. I'm sorry."

"You're sure?"

When he answered, his voice was low. "Maybe I did. Once."

"When was that?"

"Shouldn't you lie down?"

"No. And please tell me. When did you pray I would be cured?"

"The time I went to the cathedral to tell the cardinal about the condoms. Except I didn't get to the cardinal. I got to this other priest, for communion, and after I'd said it, about the condoms, he just repeated what he'd already said. 'The Body of Christ.' So I took communion anyway. And then I had to pray something. So I prayed, 'Cure her.' But that's the only time I can remember. Why?"

Dempsey nodded her head twice. Johnny could barely see her, the lighter gray of the window darkening itself to the deeper gray of Dempsey and the chair and the wall. "I will, though," Johnny said.

"No. That's all right. You can forget about it now."

"But I will —"

"No. There's no need. Not anymore."

"But it's not too late. It can't be!"

Dempsey raised her head. "I went to Doctor Norstar this afternoon. She called. She wanted to see me."

"More tests?"

"No. 'No more tests,' she said."

"What'd she want then?"

"She was moving her office. Upstairs."

"And *that's* what she wanted to see you for?"

"Everything's out of the old office. We even had to get up especially so the men could haul away the couch in the waiting room. We didn't mind. Not at all. They were very polite, the movers."

"Dempsey, Doctor Norstar did not ask you to come see her just so you'd be there for the move. Now why —?"

Before he could continue, Dempsey said, "I'd brought some colored pencils and a drawing book so if her little boy was there —"

"Dempsey, please, what did she want to see you for?"

"She told me I'm cured."

Johnny waited for her to say more, but she said nothing. "Cured?" he asked. "What do you mean cured?"

"All those tests, that's what they were for. I'm cured."

"Those tests were not treatments. They were tests. They wouldn't cure anything."

"I know they were tests. And they mean I don't have AIDS anymore. The virus is gone. That's what Doctor Norstar told me."

Johnny took one step closer, then stopped. Dempsey

went on talking. "The tests—they were to make sure. She suspected it, but didn't want to say anything—you know—get my hopes up. But now she knows. I mean—I'm negative. There's no evidence of the virus—anywhere in my body. And they looked for it everywhere. All those tests. I'm cured, she said."

Johnny waited for the streak of terror shooting through him to complete its course. To settle quietly in the ends of his hair, in the bristle of his chin. The dementia had come. Dempsey was losing her reason and nothing could stop it. The tests, the endless tests, the endless repeated tests had searched it out and had found it at last. Doctor Norstar must have seen the symptoms earlier, symptoms Johnny had no way of suspecting, symptoms in behavior, symptoms in the blood, in the spine, in the brain. And this was the chosen way for Dempsey to make it known to him. This was the chosen moment to let him know that the final horror had arrived and was dwelling in her brain. Whatever Doctor Norstar may have said, this is what Dempsey had chosen to hear and tell him. That she was cured, that she was not sick, that she would not die.

And to support her claim, she had asked him about the prayer. The connections available to the disconnecting mind, the summoned logic, the dazzling, darting thoughts, sparking from one point to another, a pattern of sanity, a web of reason in which to entangle those too stunned, too caring to make a quick escape. He must keep himself free of the web. He must not address the warped logic; he must not be deceived by the cunning patterns that disguised the madness within.

"That's wonderful," he said. "You're cured."

"You don't believe me. That's all right. I don't believe it either. But it's true."

"Why wouldn't I believe you?"

"Why should you? Why me? It can't be you and your prayer. You don't believe that, do you?"

"No, of course not." He started toward her. Dempsey drew herself up in the chair.

"Stay there. Please. Don't come near me."

"I'm not near you."

"You are. You're too close."

Johnny stayed where he was. Dempsey, he now knew, would be taken from him. She had gone mad. She would be put into the care of those trained to handle patients in dementia. He would lose her; she was lost already. His one wish would be denied. He would not be able to care for her to the very end. He might not be the last man she would see, would touch, in this life. All that he had wanted, all that had been promised from the day she let him come back to her, would never be his again. She had escaped. She had found a way to leave him again. She had retreated into herself. What he had hoped for, his great reward, would never be given to him now.

He turned away. His steps took him to the sink. A saucepan and some silverware were still in the drainer. He quietly hung the saucepan on the pegboard next to the refrigerator. When he picked up the silverware, he could feel that it was still wet. He dried it, spoon by spoon, fork by fork, dropping each piece into its proper compartment in the top drawer beneath the drainboard. He listened for Dempsey, but the clang of the dried silver was the only sound he could hear. Soon he would turn around and see where she was.

He let fall the last spoon into place; closed the drawer, folded and hung the dishtowel on its prong. He straightened out a row of glasses on the shelf above. When he turned around, he saw Dempsey sitting at the table. She had peeled an orange and was pulling one of the slices free of the others. He hadn't smelled the orange until now. Dempsey put the slice in her mouth and began chomping on it. "When I felt like Rice Krispies, that's when I was being cured. The snap, crackle, pop. Remember? The virus was leaving my body. That's why I had to lie down. It was at the same time you were praying in the cathedral. That's when it happened. I was being cured. Snap. Crackle. Pop. Like demons being driven out, God's command. 'Leave her. Leave her.' And the virus, it left me. I was cured. I am cured."

When Johnny said nothing, she continued. "Can you stay at your mother's tonight?" Her voice was low, almost mournful.

"No."

"Why?"

"I have to be here."

She was pulling threads of pulp from the separated slice. "I want you to stay at your mother's."

"I have to stay here."

"Because I'm crazy and can't be left alone?"

"Yes."

"Then call Doctor Norstar and tell her I've gone crazy and ask her what you should do. Call her."

She got up and went to the wall phone just outside the bathroom. She punched the numbers she knew so well. "She'll be at her apartment by now. Unless she's still at her new office. I wish I'd gone up and seen it. I wonder what it's like." She held the phone away from her so Johnny could hear the voice. "Doctor Norstar. Hello. Doctor Norstar." The voice sounded like someone in desperate need of Doctor Norstar.

After Johnny had heard what the doctor had to say, he hung up but kept his hand on the phone a few seconds, then drew it away. He lowered his head and saw that there was a toothpick fitted into the groove between two floorboards. He had been picking his tooth while talking to his mother the day before. "You're cured," he said quietly.

"Yes. I know."

He looked again at the phone. "You're cured." This time his voice tried to sound louder. Dempsey said nothing. He looked toward her. She was still at the table looking at the peeled orange she held in her hand. "You're cured," he said again. He moved toward her. "You—you're cured, she told me." He reached out his hand toward Dempsey's shoulder. She pulled away. "But you're cured!" he said.

"I know." Her voice was barely audible.

"Do you know what that means?"

"No. I don't know."

"It means—it means—it means you're—you're cured."

"Yes."

"But—shouldn't we do something? Say something?"

"What?"

"Something. Anything. Sing! Dance!"

Dempsey rubbed the tip of her fingers gently over the surface of the orange. "You make it sound like it's the same as something like winning the lottery," she said quietly. "Like we're supposed to yell and jump up and down and hug each other as if we were on television. But it's not the same. I'm cured. You prayed I'd be cured. And now I am. It's not like the lottery. At least I don't think it is."

Making as little sound as possible, Johnny sat down across from her. He waited a moment, then said, "You — you think — I mean — it couldn't — you don't believe that just because I prayed . . . Do you believe that?"

"Do you?"

"I don't know what I believe."

"Then can't we just sit here?"

Johnny looked over at Dempsey. She was staring. Her mouth slightly open, her eyes filled, it seemed to him, with sorrow and fear and possibly with love. "What?" he whispered.

"Nothing."

She looked up toward the ceiling. Johnny, too, looked up. The two of them, slowly moving their heads, searched the upper reaches of the entire room as if they might find there some presence, seen or unseen, some wise and gentle counsel that would explain to them what had happened and tell them what was happening now. They found nothing. Johnny looked at Dempsey's hand. She was slowly tugging another slice free from the rest of the orange. "Please say something," he whispered.

She waited a moment then said in a voice no louder than his. "Would you like some orange?"

Because he could refuse no offer she would ever make, because his love and his yearning were streaming out of him, escaping through every pore, reaching toward her, toward infinity, he said, "Yes. Thanks." She set a slice in front of him. He waited, then picked it up and put it into his mouth and held it there. He didn't want to chew, but after a few seconds, he chewed anyway.

A foghorn sounded from a distant ship. Johnny stood up and moved as quickly as he could to the outer deck. He wanted to throw up. He grabbed on to the rail and thrust his head out over the water. Nothing came. He leaned back and raised his head. "Don't let her—don't let her be cured—not by me. Not by me," he whispered. "Don't —" Again he leaned out over the rail. The water was gliding alongside the boat, thin, curled ripples the only disturbance made by the ferry's lumbering bulk. "I mean — I mean — thank —"

He hiccupped. After a held breath he tried again to say the words. But he hiccupped three times in quick succession. He looked out over the water. He saw the Verrazano Bridge; he saw Governor's Island, he saw a freighter and a container ship. One by one he looked at each of them and, as if in salute, he hiccupped to the Verrazano Bridge, to the freighter, to the container ship. He hiccupped to the water below. He hiccupped to the moon above.

10.

Dempsey was completely confused in her quest for some suitable response to her cure. Numb at first, then restless as well, she became desperate to find some task that might lead her, if not to serenity, then at least to a minimal measure of stability. When a fit of trembling came to her, her first thought was that the illness had returned. She was having the familiar chill. She would shake. Her teeth would chatter; her bones shudder, and then the sweats would come. After that, perhaps a decent sleep, some welcome rest, the wet sheets cooling against her fevered flesh.

A possible peace suggested itself. She was still sick. She had not been cured after all. It had been a gigantic mistake. Nothing now would be required of her, no word, no deed, no response at all. She could just shake and shudder away, let the sweat seep out and then be given, perhaps, some good and blessed rest. All would be as it had been. Her death, faithful at last, had returned and she found solace in the trembling that racked her now.

But the trembling passed; the stupefaction remained.

Her Lazarus painting was not a possible response. The needed concentration and energy were nowhere to be found. Her skills were somewhere, but she felt no certainty that she could find them and put them to use. To occupy herself while thinking through her predicament, she decided to scrub the floor. The entire floor of the entire loft. With a hard-bristled brush, on her knees. Without hurry, she moved paintings and equipment, furniture and rugs, plants and books. With a firm circular gesture she scoured the gray painted wood, an active froth rising as the soapy water drew out the accumulated grime and dirt that had survived the perfunctory mopping she'd given the floor from the day of her arrival in the loft. Starting at the elevator, she worked her way through her studio area, finding two paintbrushes she'd forgotten she had, one unfinished painting from six years before (not half bad, considering how greatly her work had improved since then), and seventy-six cents in change. There was also a wooden spoon she didn't recognize, possibly left behind by the previous tenant, a dead mouse long decayed, and under the rug, one of Johnny's maroon socks. She would wash it and see that he got it back.

Then she remembered the day at least half a year ago when a single maroon sock was cursed for being without a mate and thrown into the trash. She'd cared that much at the loss of symmetry. Now, without further thought, she tossed this second sock into the wastebasket and resumed scrubbing. Perhaps the scrubbing itself was the purpose for which she had been cured.

When she was about four feet from the windowed wall in front of the loft, Dempsey stopped and sat back on her haunches for yet another rest. She brushed her arm across her forehead not because her hair had fallen into her eyes or because she was sweating. It just seemed the required gesture for someone scrubbing a floor. She'd already done it more than several times while working on the vast acreage that lay clean and fresh behind her. And she would probably do it at least once more before the final patch was done.

When she leaned forward again, putting weight onto the brush, getting ready to make the circular motion, she realized that she had, without knowing it, made an uncounted number of gestural paintings in the course of her scrubbing. Monochromatic they may have been, and somewhat repetitive, but surely she had performed a major exploration of what lay within the motion of her hand, her arm, her entire body. Everything within her, all her strength, all her patience and persistence, had gone into this work. She had given it all she had to give. She was tempted to look behind her, to view her achievement, to be awed by the immensity of her accomplishment. But it had all, of course, disappeared even in the act of its own creation. The rags with which she'd sopped up the detritus of the scrubbings had erased the frothing swirls, whole skyscapes and emerging galaxies, the limitless configurations of a universe at last revealed—all lost. There was nothing but an expanse of flooring, battleship gray, marked by parallel grooves between the boards.

She finished the scrubbing. She slipped the brush back into the pail so it wouldn't splash. When she braced her hand against the floor to help her stand up, she realized that the task she'd chosen, scrubbing the floor, was a task that could be performed only on one's knees. She wanted to laugh, but nothing seemed funny to her anymore.

Dempsey's next attempt was a cliché, but clichés became clichés because, more often than not, they began as a truth: She would give herself to good works. If she were the beneficiary of divine intervention, if she was, indeed, one chosen among many, she should at least offer some token of gratitude. And if she was merely a freak case, yet one more of nature's playful little tricks, she had nothing to lose. She might accrue an even greater grace from the act since it had no purpose beyond itself. It would gain her nothing. It would simply be. The degree of merit she would leave for others to decide. She herself would just go and do it.

Her choice was an obvious one. Johnny had told her about the soup kitchen run by the good priest—Father Dunphy if she remembered correctly. It was on a specific day of the week, at a specific hour. Johnny had also told her where the church was, not too far uptown, in the Village. It was the church in which they were to be married. She would go to the soup kitchen and offer her services. It might have no effect; it might do nothing to rouse her from the stunned state her cure had inflicted, but it might be of some help to others and she had no real objection. (She recalled the words of Sister Sarah on the subject; "If you're a Catholic and you don't make the poor your first concern, you're nothing but a freeloader. To those who ignore or, worse, punish the poor, the Eucharist, the Body and Blood of Christ, becomes nothing but a free lunch. God gag them, I say.")

And so, wearing her jeans and a paint-spattered T-shirt, Dempsey dutifully went, prepared to accept whatever might happen, even though she had little interest in what it might be.

The church looked like an Irishman's idea of a Greek temple. It had fluted columns in front, but the rest was made of stones cleared from what must have been the surrounding pastures, the grazing land upon which it had been built more than a century and a half before, as a plaque informed her. The columns' claims of a lineage that went back to antiquity were allowed to grace the portico and the facade, but the actual stones must have known the rooting of cows and sheep, horses and pigs. The walls were ramparts culled from the rocky earth; a fortress for a pastoral rather than a mighty God. There was a sturdy honesty to the structure itself that suggested a homely faith hospitable to glory and to grandeur.

Along the side of the church and down the block the long line of people ran. Most were men. The dress code was obviously casual. No rags or tatters were readily visible but little thought seemed to have been given to the fit and cut of what was being worn, mostly sweats and T-shirts. The line itself was formed on a ramp coming from the direction opposite to where Dempsey stood, at the top of some stone steps that led down to the church basement. It seemed that as a volunteer she should go down the steps, through the door, into the basement, and offer her services. And she should not hesitate. The line was already moving. But she did hesitate.

A man carrying a huge black plastic garbage bag on his shoulder, the bag stuffed, it seemed, with empty beer and soda cans, was passing through the door, the man a reverse Santa Claus collecting the city's clutter, the recipient of urban largesse rather than the dispenser of unearned gifts and undeserved toys. Behind him was a woman who looked like a schoolteacher, gray hair pulled back into a bun, steel-rimmed glasses, a plaid skirt and a cardigan unbuttoned over a pale green blouse. She wore white shoes, not all that scuffed, and ankle socks with dainty pink flowers embroidered at the top. In her hand was an empty two-pound Maxwell House coffee can without a lid. Perhaps she was hoping for carry-out. Next came a teenager, a boy, with scabs on his nose and under his right eye. His T-shirt was dirty and torn at the neck so that some of the material flapped away from his chest, exposing his right nipple.

As the teenager was passing through the door, Dempsey turned away from the steps and went down the street, past the ramp, along the file of people and took her place in line. This was where she felt she belonged. In front of her were two men who stopped talking and faced front the moment she joined them. One had just said, "You can't do it that way. That way, they won't oblige. You got to get them to oblige."

Nothing more was said, as if Dempsey were there to enforce discipline and ensure proper conduct. A man singing inaudible words interspersed with an occasional "Yeah" came into the line behind her. And behind him came a young man with long hair and a vacant stare that made him look like a deposed comic-book prince who had been sent out into beggary and would never find his way back to hearth and home.

Dempsey lifted her tote bag and held it against her chest so it wouldn't rub the knee of the man behind her or hit the leg of the man in front. Why she had brought the tote, she had not the least idea. Habit, probably. There would be little opportunity for knitting or for reading the book buried somewhere toward the bottom. The clean underclothes kept there for emergencies, the shield replacements and, probably, an extra shield, which should have no purpose for her now. Nor would she ever need again the small box of latex gloves tucked in there somewhere, or the colored pencils and sketchpad she'd stuffed into the bag the afternoon she'd gone to see Doctor Norstar, hoping Joey might be there and he and she would draw together to make some peace between them. But Joey hadn't been there. Only Doctor Norstar and the movers. Chances were that she would never see Joey again; they would never draw, they would never make their peace. Dempsey hugged the bag closer.

Slowly the line moved, but steadily. The men ahead of her never spoke again; the man behind her continued his song and the interspersed "Yeah's." Since she didn't turn around, she knew nothing of the deposed prince. Dempsey did not plan to stay for lunch. She had no idea why she'd placed herself in the line to begin with, except that it seemed right. She just had the feeling she belonged there rather than among the volunteers. But to accept food seemed unfair and not far from theft.

Once inside, however, she stayed in line, accepted the buttered bread, the bowl of what looked like a barley soup with huge chunks of meaty sausage and fresh vegetables—red cabbage, carrots, and celery. She accepted the sliced peaches and the coffee. As she had dutifully waited on line, it seemed the proper thing to do. And then it came to her, that perhaps the reason why she felt drawn to wait on the line was she still didn't quite believe that she was being allowed to live.

Most of the long tables were full but she saw an empty place facing the wall in a far corner. A man with a scraggly beard brushed past her, almost knocking the tray from her hand. She brought up her other hand, the one carrying the tote bag, and reinforced her hold. The tote swung back and forth against her stomach, the bottom corner hitting her repeatedly in the crotch. She moved toward the empty chair. An older man in a brown overcoat rushed by and Dempsey was certain he was headed for the same place, but he swerved to the right and sat down in front of an empty tray on a table near the middle of the room.

The overhead fluorescent strips made the room overbright, without shadow, and Dempsey felt she was moving through air made brittle by the light. A wrong or hasty move and the air might shatter, leaving it in shards, pieces scattered at her feet. On she moved, slowly, carefully, not just to avoid disrupting the fragile air but because she hoped some mental process would catch up with her, bringing some understanding of why she was doing what she was doing. But her mind was in no hurry to go anywhere, and Dempsey herself felt no eagerness for goads and prods. She had only to keep moving, to do what she was doing, and not require anything beyond the event itself. By the time she reached the chair, she no longer cared that the corner of her tote bag had been poking her in the crotch and that she had slopped some of the soup onto the tray.

The soup was hot and the vegetables firm. Dempsey knew that a fat man who made noises when he ate was sitting across from her, a woman and a child were seated down the table, and next to her was someone who clutched his spoon in his fist and whose elbow showed through the sleeve of an unbuttoned sweater. Dutifully she ate the soup and the bread, generously buttered. As if at a signal, she lifted her coffee to her lips and drank.

Now music could be heard, far away. Someone was playing the organ in the church above. No complete measure came through the basement ceiling, only occasional phrases, as if the waves of sound were advancing, then receding, trying to draw her closer, away from where she was. The music was coming from the church where she was going to marry Johnny. The idea seemed a strange one. She knew she loved him and had said she'd marry him. She had wanted to marry him. But that now seemed so long ago and Johnny himself seemed so remote, so distant, a man from another life for whom she was desperately trying but as yet still could find no place in the life she was living now. He was the finest man she had ever known. He was probably the only man she had ever loved. He was kind, he was brave; he was beautiful and gentle; he was passionate and had rust-colored pubic hair, which seemed to her highly erotic. Johnny had taken care of her when she was sick; he would stay with her until she died. But she was no longer dying. Johnny had prayed for a cure and his prayer had been answered. She could live on and on and on. But Johnny had no purpose now.

Why, she berated herself. Why? If in dying, she had loved him, why in living did she barely know him, much less feel the depth of what she'd felt before? Why had he become undefined? Why did her need for him no longer exist? The diminishing of her feeling for him was even more of a mystery than the fact that her own death was now in the distance, as undefined as Johnny was now undefined—even up close.

It was time for another few sips of coffee, but Dempsey felt no inclination to drink. She would wait. The moment would make itself known when it arrived. She would then raise the cup, put it to her lips and take a good healthy gulp. She waited. The moment did not seem to be coming any closer. She waited longer. Maybe, if she took in a few more spoonfuls of the soup or took a bite of the bread—but no, it would be inappropriate. Dempsey continued to wait for the moment when she would drink her coffee. It seemed unfair that the signal was being withheld. Then she decided she would leave. She would submit no longer.

She stood up, took her tray in her hand, and reached down for her tote. It wasn't there. She looked under the table to see if it had slipped away from the side of her chair. It wasn't under the table. She looked around the leg of the chair occupied by the man with the unbuttoned sweater. He was young with mussed-up hair. The tote bag was nowhere to be seen. She looked behind her and in front of her and to both sides of her. No one paid her the least attention. She was about to ask if anyone knew anything about the disappearance, but she knew it would do no good. No one knew anything. The tote bag was gone. It had been intended that it should be gone. She must ask for no explanations, she must demand no knowledge. And most of all, she must not expect it back.

A rage began to rise in her. She had been robbed. Something had been taken from her. The injustice, the violence against her must not pass without protest. She would cry out; she would denounce and demand; she would accuse and condemn. But then the rage subsided before she could give it utterance. It ended as if by some abrupt command. Like the tote bag, it was nowhere to be found. She had come to this place to quietly surrender the bag, to have it taken from her and never returned. She had come among these people because they were her own. From each, something had been taken and would never be found again. The search had been long abandoned and completely forgotten. It remained for Dempsey to leave quietly, to make as little noise and move with as little motion as possible. The time had come to resume her ordinary life, her usual living. She must phone Johnny. The painting of Lazarus resurrected must be started. And finished.

Carefully she slid her empty chair back into place at the table. Her untouched peach slices she left for anyone who might want them. Looking neither to the left nor to the right, she brought her tray to the stacking area and performed the required protocols: the leftover soup, less than half a bowl, the unsipped coffee, the last morsel of bread thrown into the garbage; the bowl, the spoon, the tray deposited on the stainless-steel counter, a murmured thanks. A huge man with a great shining bald head, bent over the sinks, called back, "You're welcome. Come again," without turning around.

Dempsey walked toward the door. People were still arriving. These were the ones she should thank: these and the man with the black plastic bag, these and the man with the unbuttoned sweater, these and the woman and the child. They had allowed her to be with them. They had accepted her as one of their own, the robbed, the pillaged, the violated. As she walked through the door she murmured the words, "Thank you . . . thank you," to the new arrivals. No one seemed to find this anything but ordinary and perfectly acceptable.

11.

Dempsey and Johnny were walking past the old Custom House, now a museum dedicated to the dispossessed indigenous Americans. When Dempsey had phoned Johnny, she told him that she had finally decided to at least try to get started on the final painting of her memorial to Jamey, *The Raising of Lazarus*. She had asked if he could come sometime soon to pose, which, in turn, might help her find the truth at the heart of the miraculous event which, only she, as an artist, would know.

He'd told her he was busy repairing the roof of his mother's house. With a laugh, he mentioned that he was, during his off time, going from one task to another to keep his mind off more important things. As a matter of fact, he'd already fixed the fence that separated the yard from the sidewalk.

Now, at her request, he told her that he was on duty that evening but would come immediately and give her what time he could. He wouldn't even bother to shower and hoped she wouldn't mind.

Dempsey protested that it wasn't all that urgent, but Johnny told her he was already on his way. Dempsey said in that case, the least she could do to show her appreciation was to meet him at the ferry.

Although he didn't mean it, Johnny said, "That won't be necessary."

"That's why I'm doing it."

It pleased Johnny to say, "Well, if you insist."

* * *

When he came down the ramp from the terminal, Dempsey saw that he'd meant what he'd said. His jeans were stained with tar from the roof, great swatches across the knees and lesser splotches dabbed near the pockets and up and down the right leg. The left leg, for whatever reason, was unspotted. His T-shirt was immaculate, and she suspected he had taken time to shower after all. Her suspicion was disproved when, after a clumsy raising and lowering of elbows and hands, they'd gone into each other's arms. His body smelled like beef stew. When they'd separated for the obligatory look at each other, they avoided each other's eyes. Because Dempsey was concentrating on his right cheek, she could tell that he was examining her forehead. They'd smiled, they'd hugged once more, and they'd turned and begun their walk to the loft.

After they got to Bowling Green, Dempsey looked a little bit toward her left. Johnny was staring straight ahead. His mouth was open. Was he going to say something? But he didn't. He simply closed his mouth, then looked down at the sidewalk.

Was he as confused as she was? He had asked that she be cured and it had swiftly come to pass. Was he frightened by the mystery of what he'd done? Was he bewildered by whatever demands might be implicit in his success? Must he, like she herself, wait for some small bit of enlightenment that would show them the way out of the wilderness? Perhaps he, no less than she, had been set down in the labyrinth—not knowing how he got there or what might be expected of them now. No clues were being given, no guidance offered, no thread spun out to lead them safely back to the known world.

After they had crossed Fulton Street, Johnny, with surprising ease, said, "The word *pitch* is from tar. When we say *pitch black* that's what we're talking about. Tar. The pitch is in the tar."

Then it was Dempsey's turn to speak easily. "I found your maroon sock when I was scrubbing the loft floor."

As if not understanding what she'd said, he said, "Scrubbing the floor? You?"

"Every single inch. And I also found seventy-six cents."

"Seventy-six cents?"

"And a dead mouse. Long dead. Behind the stack of paintings near the elevator."

"Died from the fumes."

"Probably."

Johnny turned and looked at her. "What are you going to buy with the seventy-six cents?" His smile lifted the corners of his mouth, making him look like an Irish imp come to distract her mind and disturb her seven senses.

She found herself smiling back. But when Johnny saw the smile, he quickly turned away. Was he frightened at the sight of her? As frightened as she was at the sight of him?

Hesitantly, she reached up and put her hand lightly on his shoulder. After a moment, Johnny placed a hand on her wrist, gently. He waited for not more than a few seconds before slowly taking it away. Dempsey, too, took back her hand. But Johnny wasn't finished. He tried to take hold of the hand that had touched him. Dempsey drew it away.

"I can't hold your hand?"

Softly she said, "I don't know. Not now. Please." She then added, "We should concentrate on the painting."

After they'd walked less than half of a block, Johnny asked, "Am I moving back in?"

She shook her head and sadness broke over them like a burst of rain. "I don't know, Johnny. I don't think so, Johnny. And if you ask me why I don't know, why I don't think so, I can't explain because I don't know myself."

"I see," he said.

"Maybe if we concentrate on the painting?"

Johnny waited, then said, "Okay. If that's what you need." They continued on, saying nothing for the simple reason that there was too much more to be said.

12.

Father Dunphy was scrubbing the bottom of a huge aluminum pot. He stood up straight, submerged the pot into the rinse water, twirled it around, then put it on the drainboard. With a large cooking spoon he scraped the insides of the next pot, ridding it of as much rice as possible. He put it into the soapy water and said to Johnny, who was standing next to him, "Can you hear the organ from the church upstairs?"

Trying not to sound impatient, Johnny said, "Oh yeah, beautiful."

"I suspect that our organist chooses to practice on Saturday afternoons, her contribution to what we're doing."

"Nice."

"This is usually my time to myself, but for you I'll make an exception. I come down here, stick my head in the tubs so no one can see me, and don't surface until we close the place down. Nice warm sudsy water up over the elbows, time all by myself, time to think." He pointed to a dishtowel on a rack next to the sink. "Dry that and stack it there, next to the stove. Then maybe we'll see what I can do for you."

Johnny obediently began drying the huge pot, the outside first, balancing it on the table so he wouldn't have to wrestle with it. In the firehouse the cooking pots were outsized, but these were close to cauldrons. In the firehouse, of course, the cooking was for eight or nine at the most. Here it was for over five hundred and a simple saucepan would be regarded as an artifact from a distant culture.

The priest's concentration on his scrubbing was absolute, the quick back-and-forth motion with the scouring pad. It was as if he were trying to scratch through an outer layer and discover the true metal underneath, like a hidden truth. Then the broader scrape to the edges of the pot, away from himself, toward himself, all done with muscles tensed from the neck on down. The hands and the fingers took strength from the shoulders and back and pressed into the stubborn residue with a determination that could only be called defiant.

The pot Johnny was drying had a small scab of rice stuck to the side. He considered giving it back to the priest but decided that its removal should be within his competence. He picked at it, but it seemed to be cooked right into the metal. He scratched at it a bit more aggressively and what hadn't gone under his fingernail came loose. He cleared his fingernails into the pot, then upended it and let the rice fall to the floor, hoping Father Dunphy hadn't witnessed his disregard for kitchen protocol. He set the pot on the counter.

Father Dunphy moved away from the sink, took the dishtowel from Johnny, and used it to dry his hands. He draped the towel over the pot Johnny had just dried and said, "We'll eat now. And we can talk."

"I already ate."

"Eat again. Tuna Terrific. Lots of tuna. Lots of Terrific."

Johnny shook his head. "Thanks, Father, but it might cause a mild disturbance. When I came in and headed straight toward you, just about everybody waiting to eat kept saying 'End of the line . . . end of the line.' And I kept saying 'Not eating, not eating.' I can hardly go back on my word."

"Of course you can't. But I think I have a way of handling it." He drew himself up and, in a purposely pompous manner, said, "As Chief Pot Scubber, I grant you a dispensation and hereby declare null and void any and all statements by one Johnny Donegan when he said, 'Not eating, Not, eating.'" He relaxed his pose and said, "There. Satisfied?"

Johnny let out a quick laugh. "I'm honored."

"Good. Then maybe you'll honor me with your company while we both indulge in some spectacular tuna."

"Happy to oblige."

The woman serving them piled each tray with a bowl of tuna casserole, a generous helping of coleslaw, some sliced peaches, buttered bread, and a cup of coffee, black, with no sugar for the simple reason that it was not being offered by Dempsey Coates.

Places were found in an isolated, almost empty corner. The refectory table was occupied at the far end by, as heaven would have it, a man Johnny had encountered when he'd first come in, an encounter that made him feel that he might not be a welcome presence for a very particular reason.

The man had looked at him, up and down, and having observed the firemen's insignia on his shirt, had said with undisguised contempt, "You a fireman, huh?" He had then spit on the floor not far from Johnny's shoes.

Johnny considered mentioning this to Father Dunphy but then decided not to trouble him with the peculiarities of a man probably not in complete control of his faculties.

Father Dunphy and Johnny sat down across from

each other. The man who'd spit, as if in disgust, picked up his tray and moved to a table nearer the center of the room, leaving Johnny and the priest pretty much alone in their corner. Father Dunphy took no notice of the man's departure and Johnny figured he'd do the same. The priest was busy salting his Tuna Terrific. "I was wondering when I'd hear from you. I thought maybe you'd changed your mind. Or the lady had said no." He offered the salt to Johnny.

"No. I mean, she said yes.'"

"Congratulations. Tell her she should come see me, the two of you. There should be some instruction even though—I mean, considering she's sick and the time may be limited —"

The man who'd spit at him returned. "You a fireman?" he said, still more of an accusation than an observation. "You ought to be ashamed. The landlord sets fire and what you do? You go in and you drag him out. Setting fire to his own building to get us out. He's supposed to burn. It was his fire. He made it. He made the fire. But no, you go in, and you come out. And you dragging a landlord all saved. The landlord. He supposed to be cinders. But you got to get youselves a landlord. Should be ashamed of youselves."

"We rescue people," Johnny said evenly. "That's what we do. And we don't ask questions."

"Shame on you. You go rescue. Shame on you." He lurched toward the men's room, then decided to drink from the water fountain instead.

"Pay no attention," the priest said. "And about the instructions—I mean, considering —"

Johnny put an elbow on either side of his tray and joined his fingers, making a shelter for his food. "She's not sick," he said.

"She's not sick?"

"She's not sick. Not anymore."

"But I thought she had —"

"AIDS. But she doesn't anymore."

Father Dunphy put the fork full of tuna back onto his plate. "Anymore? But I thought —"

"She was supposed to die. But she's not going to die."

The priest looked at him. "Are you all right?"

"I'm all right. She's all right. She's cured."

He picked up his fork. "She's — But nobody's ever been —"

"She's cured. She doesn't have it anymore. She doesn't have AIDS."

"But from what I understand —"

"This is something you don't have to understand. Something you *can't* understand. You just have to know it."

"I see."

"You think I'm nuts, don't you?"

The priest, not without some determination, went on eating. "You could be."

"I'm not."

Father Dunphy looked down at his tray. "None of this has been easy for you—her being sick, you taking care of her, wanting to get married . . . It's not difficult to see why you might—well—why you might—"

"Go crazy."

"Or at least become a little peculiar."

"I may be peculiar, but she's still cured."

"All right. She's cured."

"Believe me or don't believe me. Talk to her doctor. She'll tell you. The same as she told me. Here's her name. The doctor. Here's her phone number." He put a folded scrap of paper next to the priest's tray, as if it were a secret message being passed from one conspirator to another. "Nobody understands it. Nobody knows how it happened. But it did."

"Maybe we should go next door, to the rectory, to my office, where there isn't so much commotion."

"Here's okay. And besides, I already told you what I came to tell you."

"Please. Let's go to my office."

Father Dunphy began to get up. Johnny reached across the table and put his hand on the priest's arm. "Father, believe me. I'm not nuts. Sometimes I think I am. Sometimes I wish I were. But I'm not."

The priest sat back down. "Her doctor—does the doctor believe . . . ?"

"Call her. Talk to her. She'll give you the facts."

"Does she say how the—the cure—happened?"

"No. She says she doesn't know. She says nobody knows. It just happened. And don't say maybe Dempsey wasn't sick to begin with. She was sick. She was going to die. But she's not sick. And she's not going to die."

Looking at Johnny with something close to disbelief, Father Dunphy said, "Are you getting ready to tell me it was a miracle?"

"No. I'm not getting ready to say anything other than what I already told you."

"But the idea of an inexplicable disappearance of the virus —"

Johnny held up his right hand. "The doctor herself refuses to make even a suggestion of anything in that direction."

"As a doctor, she can't say it, but there's no reason why I can't."

"Then say it, Father."

"It's a miracle."

Johnny turned his head away. Haltingly, he said, "If it is, I was the one who prayed for it. 'Cure her!' I was the one said it. Out loud. It's what I prayed for the Sunday you gave me Communion —"

"Johnny—you actually believe it was *your* prayer —?"

"I try not to believe it, but there it is. And I don't know what to do about it."

"Do about it?"

"I only blurted it out. I blurted it out because a couple of times—and God forgive me for it—a couple of times I caught myself almost wanting—almost wanting her to die."

"Oh?"

Johnny kept on. "If she died, she'd never leave me for someone else—the way she left me when we were first together. How could I—how could I even think it? But I did. And so I had to do it. I had to say it. I blurted it out, 'Cure her! Cure Dempsey!' I did it to tell myself I didn't really want her to die. That, and only that."

He paused then added, "I've said what I came to say. And now I'm going." He stood up. "Forgive me, but I have to get out. Fast."

"Is there anything I can do?"

"What can anybody do?"

"We can always pray."

"I already did. And look what happened."

Father Dunphy bowed his head.

A huge man wearing gray sweatpants and a dark green T-shirt with only one sleeve was standing at Johnny's elbow.

In his hands he held a tray with the remains of his Tuna Terrific. "I knew you was going to eat. Coming in, coming down the line, you said you wasn't going to eat, but now I see you. You eating more than anybody." The man laughed. "Here," he said. "Eat this." He slapped a coffee-soaked piece of bread on Johnny's tray and, cackling, went to the garbage can and threw in his tray, his plate, his cutlery and whatever food was left. His cackle rose in pitch, and the man managed to sustain it until he was beyond Johnny's hearing.

Father Dunphy didn't raise his head. Johnny took the tray to the garbage can, emptied what was left of the coffee and the soaked tuna, set the tray on the rack, and started toward the door.

The man who'd spit at him was near the entrance. He waited until Johnny got closer, then spit again, this time hitting Johnny's shoe. Johnny looked down at the shoe, at the spit, then at the man. Slowly he nodded his head. "I don't blame you, my friend. I don't blame you at all." As the man continued to glare, Johnny went out the door.

13.

The burial shroud for *The Raising of Lazarus* scratched, especially against Johnny's neck and back. Dempsey had spent almost half an hour draping the winding sheet so it would look as if he was, at this moment, bursting out of it, resurrected. First Johnny had looked too much like a Roman senator about to give a speech, then an Egyptian mummy ineptly wrapped, next a failed exercise in Red Cross bandaging.

Johnny was a fairly patient model, his patience derived mostly from the pleasure he felt as Dempsey's hands, like two small animals in pursuit of each other, fluttered and scrambled all over his body, across his chest, around his thighs, tugging, lifting, resting in the curves and angles, the crevices and hollows that would never become indifferent to her touch. Twice in her fussing she had come upon places of thrilled response that Johnny hadn't known were there—despite their unending explorations of safe sex. And once she had hit on a reflex that, through some circuitry of nerve and vein, brought excitement to his shoulder blades. He had been reminded that a knee was capable of yearning and that a thighbone could have wants that would never be satisfied. Although, since the day of her cure, she did not like him to touch her; she was obviously now allowed to touch him, but only out of necessity. This was a painting desperate to be painted.

"Can you hold it just like that?" Dempsey asked. "I won't take long." She sat down on the low stool she used when sketching and picked up the pad and pencil. Johnny tried to keep the pose, but he'd made the mistake of rising onto the ball of his left foot. His heel was off the floor and the bent toes began to ache. He wished he hadn't lifted his head quite so high. He should also have brought his upper right arm closer to his side so it could rest against his ribs. Now it was held out, half raised so his opened hand, angled toward his chest, could suggest the first moment of awe and surprise, as if he were trying to shield his heart from its own reactivated beat. If he could manage to forget that he wasn't supposed to move, he could probably hold the pose indefinitely, but as usual, he couldn't take his mind off the task he'd been given. His job was to hold still and therefore all concentration, all thought, all feeling, were given to holding still.

Dempsey's tongue was sticking out, caught in the corner of her mouth. This meant she had become completely involved in what she was doing.

Sitting on the stool, she moved her head from side to side, then looked directly at him. "Try to imagine you've been in a deep, deep sleep where you've been given a dream of the deepest contentment and peace. And now, suddenly there's a sound! A voice is demanding not only immediate and full awakening but an even more insistent command that you abandon your slumbers and surrender completely. Even the memory of the bliss is eradicated. Intrusion, disruption all senseless and beyond comprehension. Wake up! Get up! No appeal. No complaint! Arise! Arise to an unappeasable wrath!"

Two, three times, Johnny tried, but Dempsey refused to be satisfied. "Rage! Wrath! All you are is annoyed. Listen! You've been robbed! All you had been given is gone!

Never to be found again. Arise! Arise!"

Then in a more challenging voice, she said, "Have you never had taken from you all that was a completion of yourself? You experienced the complete fulfillment of all that you truly are and it's been obliterated forever! Gone! Gone! Have you never experienced that?"

Johnny slowly lowered himself off the ball of his left foot and wiped his forearm over his face. He swayed the upper part of his body back and forth three times. Then in a frightening voice Dempsey had never heard from him before, he said, "I'm ready. Are you?"

Forward his body went, as he drew himself up to his full height, the left hand held out, the right hand raised to his temple, but held away from him. He parted his lips and widened his eyes to a menacing rage.

"You're getting it! You're getting it!" Dempsey called out, "Rage! Wrath! Feel it. Know it. *Be* it!" She grabbed her sketching pencil and aimed it at the pad opened on her lap. "Don't move," she warned in a low voice. "You've got it. You've got it. Don't move. Don't move."

Johnny had found the way to hold fast, not only to his risen body but to all the anguish, all the inextinguishable rage he felt for what had happened to him and to the bewildered woman he loved with a love that gave a measure to infinity.

He could hear the rough scratch and rub of the pencil, determined and brisk lines. If the sound didn't end soon, he would go mad.

14.

The painting was finished. Johnny had come and gone from the loft for the sessions needed to complete it, when his schedule allowed. All of his attempts to persuade Dempsey to allow him to move back in were met with the repeated response, "No. I know it's terribly selfish. And it makes me sadder than anything, but I still can't say yes. I can't."

The true sorrow he saw so often on Dempsey's face shamed him, and he knew he had to give precedence to her needs rather than his own.

He did, however, have one last request. Since at the beginning of their collaboration, they had walked together from the ferry, would she—to observe the completion of their shared enterprise—walk with him back to the ferry? Her quietly amused answer was, "Of course. And thanks for asking."

Now they were in Battery Park, walking slowly toward the harbor. It would be a while before the departure of the next ferry. Johnny wanted nothing more than to do whatever he could to prolong this time they would have together. In what he knew was an all too obvious ploy, he said as they passed the pizza concession, "How about a slice?"

Dempsey, to Johnny's pleasant surprise, shrugged and said, "You want one?"

Johnny smiled to congratulate himself for his success and answered, "I won't know until I get it."

With yet another shrug, Dempsey said, "What better reason? Let's do it."

The pizza was sloppy. They had to hold it away from themselves so it wouldn't drip on Johnny's polo shirt or Dempsey's clean blouse. "They're so competitive," Dempsey said. "The pizza business. Each one keeps piling on more glop than the next. Look at this. It's intestinal. The cheese, it's like viscera. The whole mess, a surgical retrieval on a doughy crust. Ugh. Delicious." She took another bite.

They began to walk along the bench-lined path. Johnny swallowed and took another bite. The grease dripped down onto his white polo shirt. (He knew it was a polo shirt because in the place usually reserved for an alligator, there was a man on a horse, a mallet raised to strike an unincluded ball.) He aimed his crumpled napkin at the splotches, but Dempsey stopped his hand.

"Cold water. Right away."

There was a line for the water fountain. "Forget it," Johnny said.

Dempsey took a dainty handkerchief from her skirt pocket, went directly to the fountain, and stepping ahead of the line, soaked the cloth and came back to Johnny. No one had objected. She wiped the splotches, went back to the water fountain, repeated her intrusion, and gave the shirt another scrub. He could feel the cold water on his chest, running down toward his navel. He could also feel the pressure of Dempsey's hand against his chest.

A straggle of Dempsey's hair had gotten itself stuck in a gob of tomato sauce, pasting it to her cheek. It had also lengthened her lips to the smile of a clown and stained the tip of her nose as if she were being made up to play slapstick parts in a circus. Johnny took the handkerchief from her hand and gently restored her to what he considered her previous perfection.

Dempsey took their pizza remains and dumped them in the trash basket near the hot dog stand. When Johnny came toward her, she moved back onto the paved path and began walking again slowly toward the harbor. Johnny followed.

The line for tickets to the Statue of Liberty and to Ellis Island curled out of the old stone fort (which gave Battery Park its name) like the tail of a giant turtle. Two elderly men, short, with gray hair and stern faces walked by, holding hands. The wheels of a stroller sounded like the squeal of kittens being run over. A teenaged boy and girl in torn jeans and floppy T-shirts, rings in their ears and rings in their noses, were taking turns punching each other on the arm. A scrawny woman wearing sneakers but no socks was quarreling with someone unseen and a man herded four exuberant children toward the island boats, holding aloft like winning lottery numbers, the five tickets that would get them to the Statue of Liberty.

Johnny and Dempsey sat on a bench facing the promenade where the tourists had been herded together in a long tightly packed line to wait for the boats. Three men, African Americans, were entertaining the crowd with back flips—one, two, or even three and four flips in quick and daring succession. With nothing more than their will to propel them, they threw their bodies backwards, flipping themselves again and again, with a speed and sureness that for both them and the crowd were quite literally breathtaking. It was as if the immobilized tourists were being taunted for their voluntary stasis.

A woman pushing a child in a wheelchair came along the path. A bright purple balloon tied to the back of the chair kept hitting the woman on the side of her head, but she didn't seem to mind. The child, a boy, was wearing a Yankee baseball cap, the visor pointing upward, giving the child's face no shade whatsoever. He wore a yellow nylon jacket over a plain white T-shirt and big khaki pants that seemed far too large. On his feet, braced against the retractable platforms at the ends of the leg supports, were oversized Timberland boots laced to the tops and tied in large bows. The child's eyes were wide, but the face somewhat pinched. The woman pushing the chair seemed worried about bumping into something. Her eyes were watching the path and she was taking care that not even a pebble or a stone be allowed to jar the chair or its occupant. In front of the bench where Dempsey and Johnny were sitting was a discarded Pepsi bottle. The woman veered in the direction of the bench. The wheelchair, the child, the woman passed a few inches from Johnny's toes. The balloon, as if in greeting, dipped in front of his face.

It hadn't been a child. It was a young man wasted to a child's size. On his face, unshaded by the baseball cap, were the unmistakable spots and stains of Kaposi's sarcoma. His hands, gripping the sides of the chair as if he were afraid he might be pitched headlong onto the path, were already skeletal. His skin was stretched across the network of bones and the knotted knuckles. There was a quick whiff of urine, then the smell of the woman's lilac perfume. Saliva drooled down the man's chin from a slack and open mouth. The wheelchair moved on, the balloon still knocking against the woman's head.

"Why not him too?" Dempsey whispered. Her face had turned to stone and she was staring straight ahead. Johnny put his arm behind her to draw her closer. Quickly she leaned forward, away from his reach. "No. I can't. I wish . . . don't." Johnny withdrew his arm.

"Please," she whispered, "let's just sit here. At least for a little bit." She took in a deep breath, then exhaled.

Tentatively Johnny started to reach out again, but stopped himself. "Sure," he said. "If that's what you want."

Two of the gymnasts, coming toward and past each other, climaxed their act with quadruple back flips, passing each other directly in front of Johnny and Dempsey. Each of the men twisted his body in a complete turn, midair, then completed the final flip coming down on one knee, arms outstretched, head flung back. There was applause, some whistles, a few shouts. Dempsey managed a smile.

"Can you do that?" she said quietly.

"No. But I can wiggle my ears."

Dempsey managed the expected small laugh.

One of the gymnasts was passing a pail along the line of tourists, accepting contributions.

But by now the line of tourists was moving, great hordes streaming onto the boat. Most of them ignored the collection by the gymnasts, so urgent were they to embark.

The gymnast looked down into the pail he'd been passing. Obviously disdainful of the meager take, he gave one last swing of the muscled arm, flinging the coins and the few dollar bills out over the heads of the moving throng. Not many responded until the movement in the line stopped and a new crowd pressed against the barrier. To occupy themselves for the wait, they stooped and collected the scattered largesse that seemed to have rained down from the sky so they would have something worthwhile to do during the wait for the next boat out.

Dempsey stood up. "Time," she said. Johnny, too, stood up. They started along the path toward the ferry terminal.

Johnny stopped. "I'm not going," he said.

"You are," Dempsey said.

Johnny reached out toward her, but she, in turn, pulled back. Johnny let his arms fall to his sides. "All right, I'll go," he said. "But I'll be back."

Dempsey said nothing. "If I'm supposed to say goodbye, I won't," Johnny said. "I can't."

"Go," Dempsey said. "You're going to miss the ferry."

Johnny grabbed her into his arms and pressed himself against her as tightly as he could. She seemed to resist at first then closed her arms around him and held him more desperately than ever before, no matter where, no matter what. Then she pulled away. On her face was a look of terror, as if what they had done were an act more dangerous than any they had yet performed. The terror vanished, and the bewilderment. Only a small and distant sorrow remained and even that was confined only to the eyes. She looked down. "Please go," she whispered.

On the top deck Johnny stood and looked toward the promenade, beyond the line of waiting tourists, searching for the shaded seat where he and Dempsey had been, but he couldn't find it. The ferry made the turn away from the slip, the motors sounding as if they were grinding sand. He looked down into the wake of the boat. Green waves crested with gray froth streamed out behind. Gulls were searching and squealing above the stern over Johnny's head, mocking him. He saw Dempsey. She was standing near the tree where he'd slopped pizza onto his shirt. He raised his hand but didn't wave. Dempsey saw him. She, too, raised her hand, then held it there. It was as if each was making a pledge to the other, swearing an oath the meaning of which they had yet to learn.

Johnny lowered his hand and Dempsey lowered hers. He stood where he was and watched. Neither he nor

Dempsey moved. The ferry continued its lumbering way, the gulls still screeching, a sound like mocking laughter. Dempsey became smaller. And Johnny knew that to her, he, too, was beginning to disappear.

15.

Dempsey had forgotten to warn Father Dunphy that the top half of the elevator door had the habit of lowering itself about six inches in rebound after it had been raised. Now it was too late. The priest had shoved the door all the way up, slamming the top part into the frame. It had bounced back and cracked the priest's skull just above his forehead. Dempsey's cry was louder than the priest's and it was Dempsey, not Father Dunphy, who put her hand to her head in reflex against the injury.

"I should have told you!"

By now Father Dunphy was aware enough to realize he'd been hit on the head. He pressed a hand against the rising bump while Dempsey took his other hand and helped him safely into the loft. Carefully she lowered the offending door, wary of further misconduct. "I should have come downstairs myself with the elevator. It's a strange beast. I'm really sorry."

"Once, in the seminary, the branch of a tree fell on my head. Maple, and no leaves for a cushion. A real bonk. And pigeons, twice, have mistaken my balding head for a depository. I'm obviously a fair target and I won't complain. Or sue."

Dempsey led him to the couch in the living room area. "Do you want to stretch out?"

"I'm not ready for that, I hope."

"I'll get some ice."

"If it would make you feel better, but I hardly think it's necessary."

"It's necessary for me. And I will feel better."

Dempsey headed for the kitchen, the priest following. Without turning around, she was aware that he was giving the loft a fairly thorough once-over. She sensed his pause passing the worktable, his interest in the brushes she'd been cleaning, his examination of the backs of the paintings she'd turned to the wall so he wouldn't see them, then his feet on the carpet near the couch, the halt just before to look to his right and observe the bedroom, the unmade bed, the spattered T-shirt and jeans thrown over a chair with, if she remembered correctly, a pair of sweat socks, white, and some sneakers tossed near the bathroom door.

She opened the refrigerator, the freezer, and took out the ice. Father Dunphy was crossing the carpet. Now he was in the kitchen area, just at the far side of the table. The ice cubes were rattled into a zip-lock bag, the bag secured on the third try, her fingers running along the hard tubing that finally joined to seal the opening.

The priest was watching her, closely. Of that she was sure. Now he was looking out the windows. How she knew all this, she had no idea. She just knew it. Now he was looking at her again. He was staring at her hair. To take his eyes off her, he was now looking back through the loft, contemplating the distance he'd come from the elevator to the kitchen. She heard a chair scrape. He was sitting down at the table. She was relieved to remember that she'd put the snifter of pills on the dresser in the bedroom, out of view.

"You're very kind to let me interrupt your work like this."

"I was only cleaning brushes."

"Don't let me stop you."

"A break won't hurt. They can use the soak." She picked the dish towel up off the rack but decided it would be too thin, not enough padding around the plastic bag. The hand towel was better but maybe she should get a clean one—for a priest. Then she remembered: this was a clean one. She'd put it there a few hours before after smudging the other one with stains from the raspberries she'd eaten for her lunch. And, it occurred to her, she no longer needed to worry about infecting people, not that she could with a hand towel.

The towel now was neatly wrapped, the feel of the ice coming cold through the nubby cloth. Dempsey turned and held it out to the priest. Father Dunphy was eating grapes, the ones she'd bought along with the raspberries that morning. He seemed to savor the taste, his lips pushed forward as he moved a grape around in his mouth. Then he swallowed it, seeds and all. "Moscato grapes," he said. "Not easy to find."

"On Thompson Street, just above Canal."

"When I was studying in Rome I developed many tastes—or maybe I developed *all* my tastes, but Moscato grapes are near the top of the list, changing places from time to time with grappa."

"Help yourself."

The priest giggled. It was meant to be a chuckle, but it came out a giggle. "I seem to have anticipated your offer. I couldn't resist."

He took the icepack and moved it around on his forehead, then back farther, then to the side, then to the middle again until he found the bump. "Can we sit somewhere away from the grapes? I want to leave at least a few for you."

"I can get more."

"No, the seeds probably aren't good for me. But I always swallow Moscato seeds. I don't want to stop eating the grapes." He got up, the pack secure against his wound, and started toward the couch. "When you were a kid, were you given the notion that if you swallowed a seed—like a watermelon seed—a watermelon would grow inside you?"

"Of course. And I think I still believe it." She, too, managed a small laugh.

"When you think about it," the priest continued, "it was probably the beginning of our sex education—except we didn't know it." He paused at the couch. "May I sit here?"

"Please."

"I can only stay a few minutes." He sat down, but didn't lean back. "I knew I'd be in the neighborhood, more or less, when I phoned you. I'm picking up an absentee ballot at Voter Registration on Varick Street. On my way back. Going on retreat but I don't want to lose my vote. That young man coming up from Arkansas is obviously a rascal, but better a rascal than a Republican, as my mother would say. Don't let me stay too long. They close at five."

"Is that too cold?" Dempsey asked.

"Perfect. Especially on a warm day. If I were a Freudian, I'd suspect myself of having done the injury on purpose, just to get the cooling effect, to say nothing of the attention."

Dempsey sat down on the ladder-back chair and folded her hands on her lap. Father Dunphy was busy taking another look at the workspace and the canvases turned to the wall. "You're a painter, Johnny told me."

"Yes. A painter."

"And those are your paintings."

"Yes. My paintings."

"And you prefer not to have them seen?"

"Maybe you should just thank me for being spared the experience."

He laughed, then said, "All right. I do thank you."

Dempsey parted her hands then brought them together again, a gesture she hoped was sufficiently noncommittal.

"Since I've so little time," the priest said, "is it all right if I don't waste any of it pretending this is just a social call?"

"I hadn't thought for a moment that it was."

"Johnny told me about—your cure."

Dempsey waited a moment, then said, "I wish he hadn't."

"I can't say I'm sorry he did."

"Oh?"

"I really wanted to come here to—well—to ask you if there's anything I might do for you."

"It seems a great deal has been done already. But thank you."

The priest looked at her a moment. He shook his head. Some form of sympathy had relaxed his face, drawing down the corners of his mouth and allowing his cheeks to hang in small jowls along the line of his jaw. He looked away, toward the worktable. "I phoned Doctor Norstar. I hope you don't mind." Dempsey resorted again to the gesture: the two hands lifted, parted, as if releasing a bird into the air, then the hands lowered to her lap. Father Dunphy clamped the icepack more firmly on his head. "Doctor Norstar, when I talked to her, told me that because of confidentiality laws, she could not discuss your case. But she quickly added that, even if she could talk, she had no time. She added that the whole business was under continuing review and she didn't know when—if ever—there would be a final disposition of the case—" He was trying to gesture with his left hand but found it awkward, the movements angular when, it seemed, he'd intended them to be more flowing. He finally switched hands, leaving the right hand free to weave in and out, back and forth, as he talked.

Dempsey listened. She sat up straight and did what could never be less than appropriate in response to what the priest was saying, the parted hands, the return to her lap. "Nothing is ever certain, Doctor Norstar finally told me—apparently having decided to ignore the confidentiality law—until the patient is dead and there's an autopsy. And even then, according to her, the doctors could be wrong. She seemed somewhat exasperated by the whole business."

Dempsey, not wanting to repeat the gesture too often, decided to speak. "She's kept quite busy."

"I don't doubt it. But she became even more impatient—*abrupt* is the better word—when I used the word *miracle*. She very distinctly told me the word had no interest for her. It was none of her concern, she said. She would stay as far away from the subject as possible and could cooperate only in strictly medical matters, and reluctantly even then."

The icepack had slipped to the right and was no longer covering the bump. He moved the towel back farther on his bald head, but again it centered.

"What I want to do, I wouldn't want to do without your permission, without your cooperation, so I'm hoping you'll agree."

"Agree? To what?"

"I intend to go to the cardinal. I'd tell him about the

cure—the possible miracle."

Dempsey's instinct was to lean forward but she didn't want her spine to lose contact with the back of the chair.

"Miracle?"

"Your cure. Your inexplicable cure."

"Who said it was a miracle?"

"The doctor—Doctor Norstar—said there was no known explanation—"

"No known explanation—someday it could be known."

"Perhaps it's already knowable."

"More likely it's not."

"But you do believe yourself to be cured, don't you?"

"I accept what Doctor Norstar tells me. I always have."

"And you accept her inability to account for what's happened?"

"I have always accepted the doctor's inability. Yes."

"You know that Johnny prayed for your cure—"

"Yes. I know."

"The day he came to the cathedral. After I'd given him Communion, he prayed. That you'd be cured." The priest reached up and took the icepack from his head and held it with both hands against his thigh. "Johnny said—"

"You want me to take that—the ice. Father? Change it?"

"No. No it's all right." He gripped it tighter as if afraid she might take it from him by force. "What I'm saying is this: I would like to present the facts as they stand now to His Eminence—"

"You want to tell him I'm cured—and it's a miracle."

"That determination has yet to be made. I myself would make no claim. But I would like to initiate an inquiry—"

"No."

"You mean you would not cooperate?"

"I would do whatever I could to stop you or his . . . whatever he is."

"His Eminence."

"Yes. That's the one."

"The inquiry, of course, could go forward without your participation."

"Then let it."

"Why are you so dismissive of God's mercy?"

"Because maybe it isn't a mercy."

"A cure? From an incurable illness? From an epidemic?"

"But is it a mercy? I mean, why me? Why only one of us, why not everybody? All those others, they have the right to ask, 'Why her and not me? Why her and not my lover, or my husband, or my wife?' Or they could ask why are Johnny Donegan's prayers answered and not mine, all those times I said them. Or the one question I keep asking myself over and over again, "'Why me and not my son?'"

"Your son?"

In an uninflected voice, she said, "He died right after he was born. Of AIDS. I'd infected him in my womb. I killed my son. Why me and not him?"

Quietly the priest said, "I'm sorry. Truly I am. I will pray for him."

She couldn't not say it: "That he'll be cured?"

After a pause, Father Dunphy managed to say, "Does it mean nothing to you that you've been given a new life?"

"It means a great deal. Instead of a life of one devouring malignancy, I've been given a life of a different but equally devouring malignancy."

"Oh? I don't understand."

"My AIDS has been taken from me and in its place

I've been given an unrelenting sense of shame. I repeat, 'If me, why not everybody?' Doesn't anybody know how ashamed I am? That I have a shame that gives me no peace? I am in agony, even as I talk to you now. At least there were times when I could laugh at my illness. But this is nothing I can laugh at. It gives me no moment in which it is not 'Why me and not everybody?' And allow me to add that Johnny, too, as much as I have loved him, has been taken from me. Our wonderful lovemaking was in defiance of death. Now, it would be without its meaning, and I tried but I can't do it."

"But couldn't you see it all differently? Quite differently?"

"How differently?"

"Couldn't you be a sign from God that mercy still exists?"

"Me?" Dempsey said scornfully. "*Me*. A sign from God? Do you know who I am? The word *disbeliever* doesn't even begin to describe it."

In more forceful tones, Father Dunphy said, "I find *that* more convincing of what I just said than anything else you could have said. Hear me now. No one—*no one*—no matter who they are and no matter what they may have done, never—*never*—are they beyond the reach of God's mercy. Being who and what you are qualifies you more than you know to be the one chosen for an extraordinary proof of God's infinite love. Will you at least consider that?"

Dempsey stood up and extended her hand. "The ice is really melting. You should probably give it to me."

After more than a moment's pause, he held it out to her. "I assume that is your answer. I assume you prefer that I go."

She took the ice from him and said, "I thank you for coming, Father. Our conversation has, indeed, been helpful in its own way."

Without turning around, he said, "I don't suppose you'll tell me how?"

"Allow me to help get you safely on the elevator."

"Thank you."

"You are most welcome. And I mean that."

After she had closed the elevator door without mishap, Dempsey went to the kitchen and dumped the soggy compress into the sink. She tugged one corner of the towel, preparing to unzip the plastic bag and empty the water from the melted ice. Instead she reached up to the spice rack and shoved the jars, bottles and tins from one side to the other, as if working an abacus. Nimbly her fingers moved until, on the third shelf, she found what she was looking for, the oregano, a jar the size of a flashlight battery. The blue pills were inside. She and Winnie had agreed that she would not take them until she had arrived at a torment that was no longer tolerable. Father Dunphy's visit had guided her to that moment.

She unscrewed the top, looked inside and shook the jar lightly. Two small blue pills surfaced. She shook the jar again. One pill disappeared; two more came to the top. She picked one out and turned her hand at the wrist to see the pill from several sides. It was a dusty blue, the size of a lentil. A few shreds of oregano stuck to the surface. She rolled the pill between her fingers until all the oregano had dropped away. For one more moment she looked at it, then she carefully placed it back inside, letting it lie gently on the oregano like the egg of a miniature robin in a nest of dried and broken leaves. She shook the jar. The pill was still poking up through the oregano. She shook the jar again. The pill was no longer visible. She screwed the cap back on, put the jar on the shelf, and rubbed the oregano dust from her fingers into the air above the sink.

16.

Dempsey took a good long look at the painting she had finished. Lazarus indeed was magnificently risen from the dead. But Dempsey being Dempsey, she was able to find several places where more work was needed. There was that curl of hair above the left ear that wasn't right. There was no spring to it. It seemed to have been hardened by hair spray into splinters of cedar. Slowly she reworked it, giving it light and dark. A soft shadowing that finally let it touch gently into the ear. She checked to see if this should affect the lighting in the dark bowl of the ear itself or the line of hair, disheveled and spiky, that poked at the ear from the side. She had momentary doubts, then decided no change was needed. Now at last it was time to clean the brushes.

As if picking up twigs for a bonfire, she collected her brushes, gathering them into her fist until she couldn't hold any more. She slid them into the wide-mouthed can of turpentine and pressed down lightly, giving the bristles a good quick drink. She rounded up the rest: one on the floor under the table, another hidden under a putty knife she sometimes used to scrape down the smeared paint to make just the right surface for the next coat, and the last to be found was on the stool near the canvas—

the quarter-inch brush, completely worn away, that she'd used as a stick to scratch lines into the colors already layered onto the canvas. It occurred to her that a new three-quarter-inch brush would soon be needed, then was almost amused by such a needless concern.

Again she pressed the bristles farther into the turpentine, encouraging a deeper drink. Paint tubes were capped, but against her usual practice, she didn't bother to roll the bottoms or to smooth the wrinkled and dented metal. Considering the fiery burial to which she had consigned her Lazarus, it seemed only right that the flesh tones used in his resurrection were mostly Burnt Sienna and Burnt Umber.

There was nothing left in the Yellow Ochre and at first she considered throwing the empty tube away, but habit told her that there might be one last dollop inside, waiting to be forced out and given to the light. No longer susceptible to amusement, she threw it out.

One by one the brushes were cleaned, squeezed into the rags she'd set out, mostly scraps she hadn't needed for the shroud. The cloth wasn't as absorbent as she might have liked, but it would do. She rubbed the bristles into the cloth, dipped them again into the turpentine, squeezed them with her fingers, then rubbed them once more into the cloth. Next they were washed with soap and water at the bathroom sink, a final cleansing. They were dried with a clean white towel, pressed into the nap, until as much water as possible had been drawn out. If the towel showed the least streak or smudge of color, the brush was returned to the turpentine and the entire process begun again.

On a cleared space of the worktable, the brushes were lined up, not according to size or length but as they happened to be lifted from Dempsey's fist. She thought of arranging them into some kind of order, perhaps even the order in which she'd bought them—memories that, for whatever reason, caused her no effort. She could even remember something of the day itself on which each purchase of each brush had been made: a sense of the weather, some part of her clothing, an incident on the way to Pearl Paint or Utrecht or Central, or on the way home—a dog, the tubs and bins of fish in the Chinese market on Canal Street. On the day of the red sable brush—from Central on Third Avenue—there had been a sudden storm and she had kept right on walking. After she was completely soaked, she'd deliberately peed because she knew it wouldn't make any difference, wetting herself, letting it run down her legs, indistinguishable from the rain that had already soaked her to the bones. The round-tip brush still seemed to smell of fish because she'd stuck the bristle end into the bag, piercing the skin of the fish and drawing into itself forever the last oils and fluids the fish would ever produce. A man with purple eyes had sold her the two-inch brush, and it seemed only fitting that the handle, too, was purple. She never saw him again and the two-inch remained her only brush with a purple handle.

When she had finished lining them up, she counted. Forty-seven brushes had been used—one of them an oxhair, now a stub, dated back to the days of her poverty. She'd stolen it from Pearl Paint on Canal Street, slipping it up the sleeve of her winter coat. To make sure it wouldn't fall out, she'd kept scratching the back of her head so she could keep her arm raised. She'd worried that the pointed end would poke out through the elbow of the coat, but it hadn't.

The painting of the risen Lazarus she leaned against the worktable. She then placed the ladder-back chair about ten feet away. She had been told to give herself some point of concentration during the time she'd be taking the pills, some mental occupation for the intervals so she would be doing something more than just waiting for the next dose. She would look at the painting, study it, see perhaps where she'd gone wrong, or even better, appreciate what she'd done right. It would be a risky business. She might see minute or glaring failures; there would be invitations to improvement; corrections would suggest themselves. But she had determined the work was finished. The tubes were capped, the brushes cleaned, and this would have to be the end. She had forbidden herself the least intrusion now. One could, she told herself, do worse at the last than take inventory of one's flaws and failures.

One by one, Dempsey picked the blue pills out of the oregano jar. There were supposed to be twenty. After she'd picked one up, she dusted it lightly, blew on it, then carefully placed it on a saucer. There were only eighteen. She dumped the entire contents of the jar onto the table, shifted the crushed leaves and unearthed one more. She liked the idea that the final taste she would have in her mouth would be oregano. Since Johnny had scorned it as tasting too much like mud, she had denied herself the pleasure for too long. How Johnny knew what mud tasted like she never asked. But compensation was soon to be made. She would hold each pill on her tongue just long enough to catch the taste before taking the prescribed swallow of water. She asked only that the memories the taste might evoke would not be muted—the pasta, the salads, the tomatoes, the omelets, whatever.

Poking among the leaves, she found the twentieth pill. Two shreds of oregano had stuck themselves onto it and had to be peeled away. A few specks refused to go, even when she pecked at them with her fingernail. Some conjugal chemistry had been at work in the dark jar among the soft siftings, and Dempsey must honor the commitment. The specks were allowed to stay.

After she'd made a final count of the pills—all twenty accounted for—she gave the saucer a shake to set the pills in a random arrangement. Except for a cluster of four at the center, they placed themselves at varying distances from each other, with none touching.

It was while she was filling the pitcher, there at the kitchen sink, after the water had begun to run as cold as it could get, that she felt some swift unease, a mild disturbance that seemed more a shift of equilibrium than an actual physical event. She waited to see if it would come again so she might identify it. Then she realized what it was. A fire engine had sounded in the distance. She could still hear it. She held the pitcher under the running water. Another engine could be heard coming from farther south. She pulled the pitcher away, listened, then turned the water on even harder. She spilled some out, back into the sink. The pitcher was too full. The sirens had faded away.

Dempsey sat on the chair facing the painting. The saucer, the pitcher, and the drinking glass were on the stool just to her right, a little forward of the chair so she wouldn't have to twist or turn. She took off her watch and propped it against the edge of the saucer. It was already after four o'clock. She wanted to finish before dark, and the days were getting shorter. Some ginkgo trees she'd seen yesterday were already beginning to turn the lemon yellow that, for her, provided "fall foliage."

A slip of notebook paper, serrated at the edge where it had been torn away from the binding, lay next to the watch. There were the instructions. Particular care had to be taken not to swallow too many at once. She might throw up. Might pass out before the full dosage (Winnie's word) had been ingested (again, Winnie's word). She set the timer of her pill dispenser. It could chirp and beep and let her know the interval had passed; it would be time for the next "ingestion."

Winnie had been bequeathed the pills—and the instructions—from a friend who had died before he could put them to their intended use. She had told Winnie nothing of the cure: she had told her only to come to the loft late that night and make the "necessary arrangements." Winnie had started to protest, then to cry, but was reminded of their original pact. Winnie said she'd be there, obedient to Dempsey's instruction.

The taste of oregano wasn't strong enough to cover the chalky flavor of the pills themselves. She took a gulp of water and let four pills wash down her throat. She should have let the water run from the faucet a little longer. It wasn't as cold as she might have liked. But now it was time to look again at the painting.

The light came blaring from the right side onto the figure of Lazarus, an explosion blasting against his flesh. This would be the force created by Jesus's command, "Lazarus, come forth!"—a dry run for the Judgment Day, when the bodies of all the dead would be called out from the earth, from the sea, from the dust, from the fire. The word, here, would become not flesh but light, and the light itself would be the irresistible pull, up and out of the tomb.

Lazarus was twisted to the left, away from the light, allowing parts of the body to emerge from darker and deeper shadows. An exercise in good old chiaroscuro. Dempsey reveled in it and had felt herself, if not a master, at least a worthy practitioner. But it had not been the lure of drama that had prompted her to show the figure twisting away, out of the light. It was not for effect, it was not a pretext for display. This was the truth itself. Lazarus—her Lazarus—was a Lazarus enraged—a wrath she'd finally been able to instill in Johnny.

Dempsey took in the full painting. There the man was, summoned from the slumber his fevers and sufferings had earned for him. Not at all confused was he, rising here. Not like a sleepwalker did her Lazarus come forth. What she saw before her now was a ravening beast at the entrance to its lair. Unappeasable wrath disfigured his face, widening the defiant eyes, drawing taut the mouth, pulling the jaw inward. The outstretched hand shot forward to stop the light from coming further. The hand curved toward the chest was taking the aspect of a claw, readying itself for battle. Horrified that he was being disturbed at the core of his being, he was preparing to spring, to gouge and rip and shred. He was prepared to howl and roar, to curse the injustice that had robbed him of his dying and of his death.

There, behind him, was the embering fire into which Dempsey had consigned him. There, at his feet, were the ashes from which he had been made to rise. The flames, feeble now against the blaring light, still flickered against the thigh, the ribbed side, still willing to lick, to speak with a persisting tongue, telling of lost refuge, of shattered peace.

Dempsey continued to stare at the painting. She judged it to be worthy. She had feared melodrama; she'd even risked it, deliberately, but knew, looking at the painting now, that without effort she had employed an honesty that was the only sure escape from the temptations of excess. The eyes were of particular interest. Defiant, unyielding, they refused to be impressed by miracle.

Their disdain was absolute. For all the fury of the roused body, the eyes held fast to the accusation: I had prepared myself for death; I had submitted; I had accepted. I had made myself ready. In pain and in turmoil had I done this. In fear and in terror had I found my way. In grief and in sorrow I had made my lasting peace. And now I am robbed of all that I had earned. But I will not be robbed. I will not surrender my body to this intrusion. I will not receive again the troubled soul I had so freely given up. If I must rise, I rise in wrath and in judgment.

She took the second dose of pills. For a few seconds she tried to detect the taste of the oregano, but when it failed to happen, she poured some water into the glass and drank down a good mouthful. The water, this time, awakened the oregano and the taste remained on her tongue even after the pills were down.

To test the effect of the pills—if there was any effect—she looked more closely at the painting, at the details. She felt neither weary nor woozy. Patience, apparently, was part of the process. She was prepared to be patient. The painting could occupy her nicely until occupation would no longer be necessary.

Then she saw it: the left knee. Hidden, but still visible to her appraising eye was a face. In among the swirls and creases, she found first two eyes, one closed as if in a wink, then a mouth, stretched thin, then lifting to a silly grin. There was even a dimple on the chin. She leaned forward for a closer look. She blinked; she held her eyes shut then quickly opened them, wide. The face was still there. She raised and lowered her head to see if it was caused by the angle of her vision. The face, satisfied with itself, was still there, embedded in the knee. She forced herself to shift her gaze. First she looked at the figure's arm, the hand turning in toward the chest. The anatomy was fine, the gesture exactly what she'd wanted. The hand, palm outward, caught her attention before she could scrutinize the hand itself. The hand had been given particular care. Minutely she had—as a gift to Johnny—traced there the long lines of life and love, making them visible to the world, held out in proof of complex humanity. Slowly she nodded her head in approval of what she had done.

But then she detected a flaw. The lines crisscrossing each other were in a pattern suitable for a game of tic-tac-toe. There were even two *o's* and an *x* suggested in their separate frames.

Dempsey got up and rattled among her brushes. She would remove the self-satisfied face on the knee and obliterate the game of tic-tac-toe. While she was searching among the capped paint tubes, she saw her wristwatch. She moved around the table and checked the time. Three minutes and twenty-seven seconds until the timer would sound again. She would hurry and find the right tubes. She was sure she remembered what colors she'd used. When she had found the first three—the Burnt Umber, Burnt Sienna, and Mars Red—she set them near the end of the table. The beeper sounded, little chirping noises like newly hatched chicks. She went to the stool where the pills were waiting. She placed two on her tongue. She took two gulps of water. The water was getting warmer. Before she would take the pills again, she must refill the pitcher. She couldn't risk nausea. And besides, fresh water was a simple pleasure, not to be denied whatever the circumstance.

She would work on the knee first. If the face were removed, if the winking eye were obliterated, she would have no trouble with the hand.

But the face kept reappearing. No matter how thick

she spread the paint, using even the palette knife, the smile and the wink were still there. Then the palette knife slid upward, smoothing out, then burying the fine hair she'd so meticulously given to the thigh.

Again the pill dispenser repeated its bright chirp to the count of three, then three times more. The brushes she let fall to the floor after she'd used them. She wouldn't bother to clean them. Winnie knew how to clean brushes. Let her take care of them. Dempsey was unable, however, not to cap the tubes. This she did slowly, as if listening to instructions from somewhere far off. When she'd finished, after she'd matched the caps to the colors, she went back to the chair and sat down.

Dutifully she took the pills, then reset the timer. It surprised her that she didn't feel more tired. Relaxed, a little heavy in the bones, in the arms and legs, but not really tired. It was the heaviness that would probably bring her down. Perhaps what the pills did was make her that much more susceptible to the pull of gravity. Her density was increasing. Every part of her was taking on an added weight. She was pulling into herself, each organ, each muscle accepting the other as it anticipated the end.

Only her head remained light, almost buoyant. It was no trouble at all to hold it erect. It was the lightness of the head that drew her entire body, heavy as it was, upright in the chair. And her vision, she noticed, her vision was far from impaired. It seemed, as a matter of fact, to have improved. The face on the knee was gone, and on the palm of the outstretched hand, the game of tic-tac-toe was still visible, but at least now the game had been resolved. Without intending to, she had painted in the necessary *o*'s and *x*'s, giving victory to the *o*'s, a diagonal straight across the hand itself. That had not been her intention, but she was far from dissatisfied. It seemed a proper proclamation, declaring the painting finished.

Again she surveyed her work, Johnny splendid before her. Too lean perhaps, but then Lazarus was supposed to have been desperately ill. Then, too, she had, after all, reduced him to ashes. Considering the completeness of his disintegration and the abruptness of the command to get up and come out, it was no small achievement that he'd managed to be as well-muscled and sinewy as he was.

Dempsey reached out her hand. She wanted to touch the painting, to touch Johnny. She wanted to brush her hand across the hair on his chest, to feel again the light scratch, the hair springing up against the skin of her palm, a tickling that could make her body shudder. She could, perhaps, let the hand move across the body, along the shoulders. She could let her fingertips touch the lips, the eyes, cold and enraged as they might be. All would be paid tribute by her tender touch.

How pleasing it was to die. No pleasure was being denied her. She had only to seek and what she sought would be given. Her every want was being fulfilled. But then, her wants were simple and what she sought was there in front of her. But she must not wait too long for her fulfillments. The beeper would beep again and she would have to obey.

Bracing both hands against the seat of the chair, Dempsey began to raise herself. It was an effort, but she could do it. How heavy she had become. How fortunate that her head, still light, still buoyant, was helping to lift her up and allow her to stand. There was not even the need to steady herself.

But before she could advance toward the painting, she realized there was no need for her to move. Johnny was coming toward her. His hand was still outstretched, but she could tell by the moving shadows, by the flickering changes of light, that he was coming closer, that he was making his way through the patches of light and dark, past the tips of flame that sparked against his side, his thigh. There was no need for her to move from the chair. Soon he would be there, with her.

He was coming to tell her something, some message, foolish or wise, that he himself had newly heard. There, on the hand, was the message inscribed. Soon she would be able to read what it said. It had not been tic-tac-toe. Words that she must know were written there. And he was bringing them to her now. But she mustn't move. She must be where she was so she'd be there when Johnny arrived, when he will have reached her. He was advancing still. He must not tire. She was there, waiting. But he must hurry. The words, the message was for her, for her, for her.

She could wait no longer. She would go to meet him. One foot must be placed in front of the other, and she must move forward. And she must do it now.

But before she could take the first step, some chickens were hatched nearby. They had just pecked their way out of their shells and were chirping. They were hungry. They must be fed. Dempsey would feed the chicks, then she could be with Johnny. Or perhaps he would have arrived by then. The shadows were washing more quickly away from his thigh, faster the sparks flickered against the russet hair and the tawny flesh. He was almost there, the message still emblazoned on the upheld hand.

Knowing with a knowledge she'd always had, she was fully aware of how to feed the chicks. More pills were placed on her tongue. The taste was blunt and dry. So the chicks would have no trouble swallowing, she was miraculously given a glass already filled with water. Where it had come from, she had no idea; it had just appeared as if she herself had willed it. But then she remembered:

she was to be given everything she sought. The water in the glass was but a small part of a grand design of which she was the center. For the chicks' sake, she swallowed the pills.

She looked toward Johnny. But it wasn't Johnny. It hadn't been Johnny all along. It was someone else. It was not Johnny. It was not Lazarus. She raised her hand, not sure if it was to fend off the stranger or to greet him. Then she saw who it was, who it was coming toward her. It was Jesus Himself, erupted from His tomb. Fierce was His love, desperate in His longing to greet her. Had Father Dunphy sent Him? No.

She, taking the priest at his word, had summoned Him. After all, it was Jesus who had actually cured her. Her quarrel was with Him, not with Johnny. She was with Him now, face to face.

Higher she raised her hand to welcome Him. She moved her lips. She had something she must say. She must say it now. More quickly she moved her lips, struggling to bring the words up from her throat. They were rising. The words. They were in her mouth, on her tongue. The tongue was swollen with the words she now must speak. "Cure them! Cure them all!" she cried out, not a plaintive plea but a defiant demand. "Not just me! All of them—all!" The words slipped back into her throat, gagging her. But she had spoken. She had been heard. She would say no more. Forever.

Still the chicks were chirping. She lowered her hand. She surrendered. But Jesus was advancing, coming closer, the moving shadows sliding along His body, brushing His flesh, falling away into the dark. Jesus would know what to do. There! Look there! Inscribed on His hand, the message. It would surely tell her whether or not that all, everyone, had been cured. All! All! At last. To her He was coming, heedless and terrible in His love. Closer. He was coming closer. And still the chicks, newly hatched and hungry, chirped on. But she knew she had nothing more to give.

Epilogue

If the air itself wasn't cool, it at least carried the scent of a breeze. It smelled of water, of the harbor, the upper bay, and this by itself evoked a clearer air and a cooler night. Johnny caught the scent of salt and oil that reminded him that he was an island dweller, the sea was near. Rotting seaweed was, to him, a cleansing odor and he could breathe in the stench of the most stagnant cove and feel himself renewed.

As he approached the loft, he slowed his walk, not just because he was weary, but to give himself a chance to take in the brackish welcome that gave sustenance to his spirit.

He had come because he was desperate to see Dempsey. The desperation had begun that afternoon with his rescue of a woman in the Lunch Room, the shooting gallery where Dempsey had gone for her drugs during the time of her addiction. At one point during the rescue, he'd had a fleeting thought that the woman might be Dempsey herself. This was, of course, ridiculous. The woman, after all, had been unidentifiable in the smoke and darkness, but being where he was, Dempsey was very much on his mind.

Helpless against it, the thought developed into an obsession that demanded that he see her, not in his mind's eye, but in the flesh. A part of him knew that this was not a rational determination. But because it was an obsession, it was not being responsive to intelligent consideration. No matter how absurd his need, no matter how resistant Dempsey might be, she had to respect his implacable demand.

The hospital had wanted to keep him overnight, but he'd signed himself out. He was experienced enough to know that his lungs had been as cleared as they were ever going to be. The gray snot had finally stopped streaming from his nose.

Reporters and TV cameras had been waiting outside the hospital to harass the fire's hero, but they had been forbidden entrance to the emergency room and told that John Donegan would not be released until the next day at the earliest. The cameras had left, but one reporter—*dogged* was the word inevitably used—remained, making jolly conversation with the triage nurse.

Johnny's cuts had been scrubbed and disinfected and scrubbed again, mercilessly, pitilessly. They were irrigated; they were soaked through with a searing solution. That would surely cause any surviving microbe, bacteria, or virus to die not from defeat in equal combat but from the sheer pain being inflicted. No organism could survive the treatment given Johnny's hands. Injections, too, were administered. These, he was assured, would neutralize any foreign substances that might find their way into his blood through the cuts and gashes made by the discarded paraphernalia littering the Lunch Room floor.

"Wait a couple of months," the doctor had said. "Then get an HIV test. It'll be negative. We're not worried ourselves, but it'll give you peace of mind. Strictly routine. More for you than for us."

When the doctor had repeated his assurances the

third time, his voice more casual with each repetition, Johnny felt that this was a memorized exchange that had no real meaning. He had his response ready. "I will. Definitely."

After his hands had been thoroughly bandaged and the steroids emptied into his system, he had argued with the doctor about his release and signed the official forms relieving the hospital of responsibility. A nurse, older, somewhat squat and wearing a black leather vest over her hospital whites, had showed him a door at the back of the emergency room that led to a corridor. She pointed to the left and said, "That way and you're out."

Johnny had hurried along the corridor and continued on to the promised exit. He thought he could hear someone approaching from behind, the dogged reporter probably or some officious hospital administrator who had found, among the intricacies of his signed form, an unnoted legalism that invalidated his release. He reached the door and leaned against the crossbar. He stepped out into the sea-scented night and began his walk to the loft.

With the tip of his forefinger peeping out of the bandages, he pressed Dempsey's bell. The pressure, slight as it was, pushed itself into his hand and it seemed that all the wounds had been forced open, that the crusted blood had cracked and split, that new blood would soon seep through the layered mitten of gauze and tape.

During his walk from the hospital, a teenager, a truck driver at a stoplight and a long-haired man walking a dog had, in irresistible inspirations of originality and wit, said, respectively, "Put 'em up, slugger," "Ready for round three?" and "Like your mittens, man." Johnny, too tired to comment, too eager to get to Dempsey's, had chosen to ignore each offering to the sum total of the world's wit as it was made, and had kept right on walking.

The teenager had giggled, the truck driver guffawed. Only the dog walker accepted the silence his statement deserved.

The fire itself had not been that threatening to the fire fighters, even though most of the building had been gutted. When a piece of machinery, something presumed to be the size of a printing press, had crashed through from the fourth floor to the third, the lieutenant had shouted the order to take up the line and get out. Johnny, Acosta behind him, started to work immediately and managed an orderly retreat without either of them stumbling or getting tangled in the hose.

Out in the street, Johnny pulled down his facepiece and took a good clean breath, then another. Midway through the third breath he noticed the iron door with the razor wire across the top. He hadn't recognized the building until now. This was the Lunch Room. He jumped over the crisscrossed hoses and pushed against the door. It clanged open.

Johnny started down a gangway. It passed under an overhang of the first floor that led to a small courtyard in the back of the building. A door that might lead into the basement was nowhere in sight. He scanned the brick wall. Chipped white paint covered the bricks up to the first floor. There were no windows on his level. No doors. He looked up. Iron shutters were closed on all the windows above, the smoke leaking out around the frames, unable to blow out the heavily rusted metal.

As Johnny watched, the smoke began seeping out around the shutters of the first-floor windows. The fire had broken through from the floor above. It had come downward one floor at a time. The basement would be next. But he could find no way into it. Could he have been mistaken? It might not be the Lunch Room after all. That had not been the iron door Dempsey had shown him.

There was a muffled crash high over his head to the left. He looked up, but nothing had changed. The smoke still seeped, faint wisps rising easily into the air above. As he brought his gaze back down, he saw what could be a space at the far end of the courtyard, what seemed an indentation between this building and the next. Another crash was heard, less muffled, followed by what sounded like a rain of pebbles. The smoke around the window frames was getting thicker.

Johnny finally found a door in the recess around the corner of the building. Maybe this was the Lunch Room? But it was locked. Contradicting his instincts and his training, he was about to declare himself satisfied that no one was inside when a thought flickered through his mind. It was so swift, not even an instant, come and gone, a spark extinguished before it could flame forth. Dempsey could be inside.

He knew this couldn't be true, but now, unbidden, he could see her. She was there, helpless, the last breaths scorched with smoke, the struggle lessening, the mind, the effort dimming. Soon she would breathe her last. She was on the floor, one arm reaching toward the door. She would not be wearing her painter's jeans or her sweatshirt. She would have dressed for the occasion, for the Lunch Room, in her black slacks, her white silk blouse with the floppy collar. There would be the speck of blood, just below the crook of the elbow, where the drug needle had stuck, the smoke hovering over it, licking it, tasting it.

Johnny kicked at the door. It rattled but didn't open. Twice more he kicked, then a third time. He considered going back to the truck for a crowbar, but couldn't afford the time. On the fourth kick, the door opened and Johnny's foot slammed itself down just inside the room. A billow of smoke charged at him like a dragon come to protect its horde. A man, coughing, hacking, rushed past him, then another.

"Anyone in here?" Johnny yelled, but the men had disappeared around the corner of the building. He slipped his mask back over his nose and mouth and turned the screw that let the oxygen flow. He squatted down and moved into the room, bumping into a chair, a table leg, what seemed like a small cabinet.

He quickly dropped onto all fours, then lowered himself down on his stomach, keeping as close to the floor as possible, where the smoke wasn't as thick. He swept his arms along his sides to make sure no one had fallen. His hand whacked a couch, then hit something soft.

Someone was there. It was a woman. He had felt her breast. The alarm on his face piece sounded. His oxygen was out. He slid the mask down and realized he'd lost his gloves somewhere. Maybe he had left them on the truck. He had no time to care. He shoved his arms under the woman's back and pulled her toward him. There was a grunt as she tumbled down onto the floor.

Johnny could have stood up, lifted her, and carried her to the door, but that would be through the thickening smoke filling the room. He hooked his hands under her arms. Still on his stomach, he lowered his head and dragged her toward the door.

Again a rumble was heard over his head, louder, and Johnny thought he could hear the straining of wood against wood. The ceiling could go at any time. A spattering of plaster was already sifting down. He could feel his throat, his chest, being rasped more and more by the smoke, the heat digging into the raw flesh of his mouth, the taste of charred plaster on his tongue.

Someone lurched against him, hitting his shoulder, knocking his nose into the woman's hair. From the side of his eye, Johnny saw a figure stumbling out the door, yet another man.

Johnny kept his head low. His breath was short gasps, his nose still buried in the woman's hair. Now they were out the door of the Lunch Room. Johnny looked down at the woman. Of course, she was not Dempsey. She was not nearly as beautiful. He easily lifted her and carried her through the courtyard and through the iron door topped by the razor wire.

His arms were limp at his sides, his chest heaving slowly and deeply. Johnny watched the stretcher being slid into the ambulance and the doors slammed shut. The ambulance's siren screech had begun to fade when a TV reporter and cameraman behind him came toward Johnny.

"Why? Why?" the reporter asked. "Why did you risk your life for a lousy dope addict?"

Johnny, gray smoke-filled mucus running from his nose, hesitated. Then he grabbed the man by his lapels and shook him mercilessly, furiously. As the man's head snapped back and forth, Johnny spat out the words, as close to a shout as he could manage, "Because we rescue people! That's what we do! We rescue. You got that?"

A cough choked off his words, but he kept shaking the man, struggling to say more. "What we do," Johnny whispered. "We rescue."

The man pulled himself free. Johnny saw that the lapels where he'd grabbed him were soaked with blood. He looked down at his hands. Blood covered them, some of it already caked. Slowly he turned his palms upward.

Enough of the blood had been wiped off onto the reporter's lapels for him to see the scored crosshatching of cuts, some deeper than others, some a straight gash, others jagged. Blood was still slowly pulsing from some; others were crusted over.

No buzz came back to unlock the downstairs door to the loft. He could, of course, use the key he'd kept except he'd have trouble negotiating with his mittens on. He pushed the buzzer again, this time harder. It seemed to hurt less, to do less damage to his mangled hand. Or, perhaps, all the cuts were already reopened from the first push and no more injury could be done.

Again there was no sound in return. He'd wait. He went to the curb and looked up at the windows. Whether they were dark or not, he couldn't say. The thrown light from the streetlamp reached upward and cast a dull glare against the glass. There could be light inside, or it could be the streetlamp. He went back to the door. Three times he rang the bell. Three times there was no response. He'd use his key.

But when he reached down to put his hand in his pocket, he became newly aware of his bandages. Dempsey must never see those bandaged hands. She must never know that he had been cut and pierced by the syringes, needles, and vials on the Lunch Room floor. Never would he confront her with the truth of what was happening to him, that he would become ill, that there would be no cure for him and he would die. No matter what the doctor had said, his body had spoken and he had heard.

Johnny stiffened where he stood. He took in half a breath, held it, then breathed out. He lowered his head. Had he done this to himself to make certain Dempsey, cured, would never leave him? Had he dismissed his knowledge and his training, taken absurd risks that were more a certainty than a risk, to secure her devotion and her care for the rest of his life? Had his rescue been not a saving act but a cowardly demand?

He shook his head, not to deny the possible truth of what had come to him but to rid himself of thoughts that appalled and horrified him. This could not be. Again he was in the blinding dark and threatening smoke. Again he made his search, his hands sweeping the littered floor. Did he know he had taken off his gloves, that his hands were being bitten and chewed and bitten again by the broken vials, the dropped syringes? Did he know where he was and what he was doing?

Again Johnny shook his head, this time slowly, this time searching for a truth he had to find. Now he stood still, his head still bowed. He waited to hear what he might hear, to see what he might see back in the dark and the smoke, to know what he must know. Then in his review he heard the woman's breath, the murmured sounds. She was there; she must be saved.

Johnny halted his thoughts to allow for a moment when he might have known he was doing some deed beyond rescue, that the rescue had been only a pretext for some other purpose he had taken no time to articulate. The knowledge, the truth must come—and it must come now. Johnny waited. The woman's breaths were heard again. He had come to the couch. He was touching her breast. He had known nothing of his hands, had felt nothing, not even the absence of his gloves. Now she would be saved. And he himself was saved. No accusation could be made against him. No motive but rescue had been in his mind. Or in his body.

Johnny raised his head and looked up again at the

dark windows. His cuts were throbbing, pulsing, as if his heart had slipped down into his hands. His neck ached. The pain was spreading to his shoulders and working its way down his spine. If he were to call Dempsey's name a window would open and she would be there. He would go up and she would see his mittened hands. She would unwind the bandages. The sight of the pulsing, crusted blood would not frighten her. She would want to kiss the wounds, but he would draw his hands away.

And then she would tell him: for this she had been cured. For this the miracle had been granted. She would be at his side, and she would care for him as he had cared for her. His sufferings would be his joy because she would be with him, his fevered rages calmed by the sweetness of her hand, the tenderness of her touch. The pain could come, the madness even, and she would not abandon him. Together they would exult in the presence of God's mercy, at this revelation of his mysterious ways—he had guided them through the labyrinth of his favor. He had bestowed on him, on Johnny, a gift beyond asking. This was the true and final answer to his prayer.

He stepped back two steps and looked up at the dark windows. He would call her name; he would be given her help. But instead he simply stared a few moments, then slowly turned and began a slow walk down the street. He would not let Dempsey see anything. She had been given her life. It was hers. It had nothing to do with him.

He raised his hand, repeating the salute each of them had made as pledge to the unknown when the land was receding from the ferry as it moved through the churning waters, widening relentlessly and irrevocably the world between them. He held the hand there to make sure the pledge had been renewed, then lowered it. The throbbing had become more a pounding than a pulse.

To its insistent beat he managed an almost stately step as he went down the empty street, continuing on his way, knowing now only too well where it would lead.

This was in the Year of Our Lord one thousand nine hundred and ninety-two.

Acknowledgments

My thanks to Lori Milken, not only for publishing this book, but for her thoughtful comments that helped me improve the text. I am also grateful to her for Joseph Olshan, the editor who brought to the task not only his exceptional skills, but an uncommon depth of commitment. Then, too, I am lucky to have such an energetic and encouraging agent, Caron Knauer.

Also the book could not have been written without the generous help from these knowledgeable people: Dr Jill Nord, who was in the infectious diseases unit at Saint Vincent's hospital, Lt. Jim Sheridan of the New York City Fire Department, and Carole Spinelli, R.N., from Saint Vincent's supportive care program for people with AIDS. My gratitude to them is beyond measure.

And thanks to my nephew, Jim Smith and his computer, and to my friends, who read and responded to the manuscript, during the various stages that led to its completion: David Barbour, Daniel D'Arezzo and Mark Nichols. With all this, it's hardly surprising that I continue to consider myself the most fortunate writer I know.

About the Author

Joseph Caldwell is an acclaimed playwright and novelist who was awarded the Rome Prize for Literature by the American Academy of Arts and Letters. He is the author of five novels in addition to *The Irish Trilogy*, a humorous mystery series featuring a mysterious and obstreperous pig. His most recent memoir, *In the Shadow of the Bridge*, was published by Delphinium in 2019. Caldwell lives in New York City.